Stay for Love

KATHERINE KARROL

Chapter 1

AVA BARTON TWISTED HER ring as she stared at the notes in front of her. Despite committing every detail to memory, there was something helpful about looking at the words again. The fact that the piece of paper hadn't disintegrated was shocking, considering how many times she had studied every bit of information on it in the last month.

"Mom, look!" Oliver pulled her out of her ruminations when he brought the picture over to where she sat on the bed. "I drew the snow outside."

"Wow, you did a great job!" She pointed to the blob in the center of the page. "Is this going to be a snowman?"

The five-year-old wrinkled his eyebrows together as he looked at his drawing. "It's a snow baseball."

"Oh, of course! Now I see it." Only Oliver would combine snow and baseball. Since receiving a mitt, bat, and ball for his birthday three weeks ago, he could combine just about anything with baseball. Snow shouldn't have come as a surprise.

He peered over at the paper in front of her. "Are you still looking at that?"

"Yes." She swept his hair away from his forehead. "I'm almost ready."

"When are we going to go for our adventure?" His eyes shone. He had been giddy at the prospect of exploring the unfamiliar landscape beyond the hotel window, especially now that snow had begun falling. No doubt he was also catching on to her stalling tactics. He was more than ready to get out of the room after being there for three days.

"We'll leave in a few minutes. Go potty, then we'll go."

He obediently trotted toward the bathroom. *Such a sweet boy.* He had exercised far too much patience while she made excuses to stay in the hotel. Even a five-year-old could only go to the pool so many times.

She paced the length of the hotel room, hearing her mother in her head telling her she was going to wear out the carpet during her stay. What would her mother think of her reasoning for making this trip if she were alive?

Shoving the thought aside, she put on her shoes. She had a mission to complete, and it was past time to do what she had come to northern Michigan for. The first day they had arrived, she had told herself that they needed rest after the long days of travel. The second, she had told herself she needed to study the document in front of her again before she ventured out into the strange world she had invaded—Jack's world. Today she had no excuses. It was time to leave the room and find him. She didn't spend two days driving from Florida to stare at the walls of a hotel room, and Oliver was getting antsy.

She picked up the precious paper and started toward her purse. It was as if an invisible wall suddenly appeared and stopped her—a wall constructed of solid panic.

I can't just go looking for him. What if I don't find him?

What if I do?

She sighed and slumped back to the bed, pretending to adjust her shoe while trying to get her head on straight. What exactly was she going to do if she found him?

Oliver watched her with questions in his eyes as he fastened the strap on his sneakers. He was definitely onto her.

The text message alert sounded, and she swiped her phone open to see the third message in as many hours from her best friend. Sarita wasn't going to back down, and Ava didn't want to worry her. She held up a finger. "Just one second. I just have to answer Auntie Sarita." As she started to reply, an incoming call popped up on her screen.

She hooked her earpiece onto her ear. "Hi Sarita. I thought you had a busy morning today."

"I did, but that was hours ago. I'm grocery shopping now, then heading home. What time zone are you in again?"

"Same as home. We drove straight north, remember?"

"Then why did you—wait a minute. Don't tell me you haven't left the room yet."

Busted. Ava squeezed her eyes shut. "Okay, I won't."

Sarita groaned. "I knew I should have made you take me with you."

She forced a normal tone to her voice, as much to convince herself as Oliver and Sarita. "We were just about to walk out the door before you called." *Not technically a lie, but . . .*

"I can have a plane ticket in my hand in an hour if you need me." Sarita was not as easily fooled as Ava might have hoped.

She smiled into the phone. "You're a great friend. I'm fine, though."

"Maybe this wasn't the best timing for this trip. You've lost your mom, your home, and your business in the last two months. If it's too much to see him now, it's okay."

Rather than bad timing, all the losses made it a perfect time to make the trip. "It's not too much. The insurance company is paying for us to live in a hotel anyway, so why not do this now?" Until the building that housed both her apartment and her gift shop was restored, there was nothing else she could do. It was the right time for this. She needed it. And someday she would tell Oliver about the real reason for their Michigan adventure.

"We're ready to go. Walk us to the car."

"You've got it, girl."

Her hand shook as she once again gathered her belongings, but having her best friend on the phone and her son staring at her with hopeful eyes helped push her to the exit door.

A bitter wind gust slapped her cheek when they walked out the side entrance of the hotel. "Oof! The wind here is as bad as any tropical storm, but it has snow in it." Oliver held tightly to her hand while he tried to catch snowflakes on his tongue.

Sarita's voice was barely audible over the wind. "Is it beautiful?"

She gazed at the whipping snowflakes. "It's gorgeous. The temperature really dropped today, though. Our Florida blood isn't used to this." When they ran to her car, she narrowly avoided falling on the pavement. Why had she put off getting proper footwear? She should have known better, traveling to Michigan in November, but the events of the last two months had thrown her off. Once in the shelter of the trusty Camry, she turned on the ignition and cranked the heat to the highest spot on the dial before making sure Oliver securely fastened his seat belt.

"Give yourself a pat on the back for getting to the parking lot."

"I know you're kidding, but I do deserve something for that. I felt like there was a force field keeping me in the room earlier."

"Well, there's nothing stopping you now. How far did you say the hotel was from his town?"

"Twenty minutes, give or take a few. At least that's what it looked like on the map." She attached her phone to her dashboard mount and opened the navigation app. "It says Hideaway is . . ."

She froze. "It's only ten miles."

Could she do this?

"Talk to me, Ava. Your voice just totally changed when you said that." Her friend's concern was a comfort in the slowly-warming car.

"I'm okay. I'm just . . . I don't know." *I don't know if I can do this yet.*

"That's why I'm here to help you. You need to take baby steps."

As she warmed her hands by the vent, she wondered if she had taken too big a step by driving all the way to Michigan. After all she had been forced to deal with in the past two months, she was about stepped out. "Okay, baby steps. You're right. Maybe I'll just drive to his town today to see where it is. We both need some warmer clothes."

"Now you're talking! Shopping would give you a destination and something to do. If you feel like going back to the hotel after that, you can do it knowing that you accomplished something big."

That sounded like something she could do. She grinned. "You're brilliant. You should be some sort of life coach or something."

Sarita's throaty chuckle reverberated through the earpiece. "Buy me lunch at Pedro's when you get home if they're back open by then. That will be my fee."

"You're on." Ava looked around the parking lot and noticed people driving slowly. They were nothing like Florida drivers. As she pulled out of the parking spot, the car moved funny. She hoped that didn't mean something was wrong with it after the big trip north.

"Okay, I'm pulling out of the parking lot. Baby stepping like a big girl."

Sarita muffled a laugh. "Baby stepping like a forty-year-old."

"Hey, don't rush me! I've got three weeks before you get to call me that." She didn't need reminding of the big four-o birthday that was coming. There was already enough on her mind.

The clouds were thickening and the snow was getting heavier as she made her way down the two-lane highway. "I need to let you go so I can concentrate on the roads."

"Okay, be careful and call me later."

"I will."

"And Ava? Operation Find Jack is officially underway. You're doing it, girl!"

Wow. She really was doing it. She was actually driving to the town where he lived. *Lord, please show me if this is a mistake. I don't really know what I'm doing here or what I'm going to find. Maybe it will be enough to get a look at his town and call it a day.*

In the meantime, she had some shopping to do. Unless she planned to turn around immediately and return to Florida, she and Oliver needed a few things—starting with gloves, judging by how long it had taken to warm their stiffened fingers.

"Are you warm enough back there?"

"Uh-huh."

A quick glance at Oliver showed a boy riveted by what was happening outside the window.

The snow increased as the navigation app took them over hills and curves and past a large blue lake, toward the town of Hideaway. It was a beautiful scene with the fluffy flakes sticking to the enormous trees that lined the hilly highway.

"Mom, we're in a snow globe!"

"It sure looks like it, doesn't it?" The driving was a little scary, but there was no denying the beauty.

"I love Michigan."

"Look at those big trees." She pointed out the window. "They look like giant Christmas trees, huh?"

"This is so cool! I'm gonna draw the trees and snow when we go back to our room."

Unfortunately, the snow also stuck to the road in front of her, making it hard to see the lines. Dodging retirees with terrible depth perception in greater Miami had taught her well, so she could handle a little bit of snow. How different could it be from the torrential rain she was used to? There weren't many other cars on the road here in the boonies, so at least she didn't have to worry about someone suddenly slamming on the brakes or cutting in front of her.

After driving over several rolling hills, she approached a big white gateway that stretched over the road. It was anchored on the ends with two large white lighthouses and had a beam connecting them with "Welcome to Hideaway" scrawled across it. *Kind of quaint. I like it.*

"Look at those lighthouses, sweetie. You can draw them later too."

"Yeah! I'm gonna make them green, though."

"No surprise there." Oliver's favorite color was green, so most of his pictures had something green, whether it was a tree, grass, or even a dog. "Look at this little town!"

The hill the gateway sat atop was the last one, and the town waited below. Off in the distance lay Lake Michigan. She had wondered what it would look like up close, and from this vantage point with the water stretching to the horizon, it looked more like the ocean than any of the lakes she had been to. The familiarity of the view helped her to feel slightly less out of place in the foreign town.

"Wow, look at that, Ollie."

"Is that the ocean?"

"It looks like it, doesn't it? That's Lake Michigan. Remember we saw it on the map?"

"It's big."

A billboard ahead with a picture of two men stole her attention. She inhaled sharply, her breath captured by the faces of the smiling men on the sign.

It's him.

When she finally tore her gaze from his face, she noticed that the speed limit drastically reduced ahead. Never one to flout a rule, she hit the brake.

The car pulled to the left. She turned the wheel, trying to straighten it out. Instead of following her direction, it kept going. *No, no, no, no!*

"Mommy!"

"Hold on, Ollie!"

She pressed the brake as hard as she could, but the car started spinning.

"Mommy!"

"Please, Lord, help!"

Chapter 2

MAX BRODY WAS ON his afternoon patrol around Hideaway when movement up ahead caught his eye. A car started fishtailing as it barreled down the big hill.

"Everyone forgets how to drive in the snow." He slowed down when it started spinning. "Lord, help that person get control."

He winced when it slid sideways down the short embankment at the bottom of the hill, barely missing the power line. "Nope."

Thankfully the car didn't flip when it jerked to a halt at the bottom, and it came to a stop in a clearing without hitting anything more than a stray branch or two. There probably wasn't any damage, so there was no need to call any backup or emergency responders. He turned onto the side street and parked near where the car had come to rest.

As he approached the vehicle on foot, he couldn't see the driver. A closer look revealed a woman hanging over the console, rear end in the air. His feet moved into high gear and he yanked the door open.

"Are you okay, ma'am?" She ignored him, instead working to get a crying boy's seat belt unbuckled. Max ran around to the other side of the car and freed the boy, who immediately went into her embrace while she hung between the seats. Slowly the woman raised her head and looked at Max, dazed.

"Everyone okay?" The air bag hadn't deployed, and neither of them looked injured.

She nodded slowly, more focused on making sure the boy was okay than answering his question. She sat back in the driver's seat and pulled him onto her lap, soothing him while he caught his breath. Max walked back around to the driver's side door. Her dark hair matched the boy's, so they were likely mother and son. Why didn't they have winter coats on? It was only twenty-nine degrees, and that was without wind chill. He looked more closely at her eyes and sniffed the air to see if she had been enjoying any afternoon cocktails. That would explain the speedy entrance into town that endangered both of them along with everyone else who might have been on the road.

"What happened?" Her green eyes were clear and she didn't appear to be intoxicated, but she was obviously shaken.

"I was about to ask you the same question." He continued his assessment. Her pupils were the same size and weren't dilated. That was a good sign. "Did you hit your head?"

She shook her head, staring down at the boy. "No, I'm okay. Did you hit your head on anything, sweetie?"

The boy's negative response was barely audible against her chest. Max needed to see his eyes too, but he would give him another minute to settle down.

"You were going pretty fast down that hill."

Her eyes flashed in irritation as she rubbed her son's back. "I was driving the speed limit, officer. Something must be wrong with my car."

He worked to keep a straight face. *Slick pavement and bad driving are what's wrong with your car.* "In conditions like this, the speed limit is ten below the posted speed."

She groaned. "How is anyone supposed to know that?"

"Driver's training. Can I see your license and registration please?"

She reached around the child clinging to her to reach her purse. After handing the documents to him, she leaned against the headrest and sighed. "Am I going to get a ticket for going the wrong legal speed limit?"

"We'll see." He tried to restrain his snicker when he glanced at the ID. "Florida, huh? That explains it."

She lifted her head. "I'm really sorry, officer. I've never had so much as a parking ticket." She looked like she was about to cry. If that was a ploy to get him to send her on her way with a wink and a smile, she was about to find out that those pretty-girl tricks didn't work here in the north.

"Stay here. I'll be right back." He walked toward his car to run her ID and check for any active Amber alerts. She seemed honest, but he didn't make the mistake of believing people were as they seemed anymore. After going down the embankment, she needed a moment to calm her nerves anyway. The way her hands shook when she handed him her ID couldn't have been just from the cold.

Her driving record was as spotless as she had claimed, and there were no alerts that even remotely matched the boy. As he approached her car, he noticed that the front wheel was bent at an angle. When he bent over, he saw she had hit a stump. So much for letting them on their way quickly.

"Do you want the good news or the bad news first?"

The look on her face gave a hitch to his gut. Maybe he shouldn't have made a joke when she was so clearly shaken. He put his hands out, hoping to calm her. "I'm not giving you a ticket, ma'am. You just need to slow down and exercise more care when the roads are slick like this."

Her shoulders visibly relaxed as she let out a sigh. "Thank you."

"Your car, on the other hand, is not so lucky."

"What? How can you tell?"

"If you want to step out of the car, I'll show you."

"Ollie, you sit over here for a minute." She patted the passenger seat. "I just need to look at the car, but you need to stay here where it's warmer. You can watch me through the window, okay?"

"Yes, Mom." The boy moved over without taking his eyes off her.

She followed Max around to the passenger side. Before he had a chance to point out the damage, she groaned and bent forward to examine it more closely.

"Oh no." She stared at the wheel. "I knew I shouldn't have left the hotel room."

"I can have dispatch send a tow truck over here to get you out of this and get your car to a shop." He gestured over his shoulder toward Woody's place. "There's one just down the street."

"I don't suppose there's a way to do a rush job on that." The way her eyes darted around and kept looking behind him made his antenna rise. Why was she so nervous?

"I can't make any guarantees, especially on a day like today, but I'll put in a good word for you." The smile that was meant to put her at ease was met with a frown.

She was starting to shiver, and rubbing her arms didn't seem to be doing much to help. Her thin sweater and jeans were not going to keep her warm with the snow and wind whipping off the lake.

"Ma'am, do you have coats in the car?"

She shook her head. "We were coming into town to buy some warm clothes when this happened."

Her lack of appropriate clothing and jumpiness since she had gotten out of the car made him wish that he had been able to get more information from the check of her driver's license. She acted like a woman with secrets, and he had a town to protect.

His radio had been quiet since he had pulled over to help them, so he had a few minutes to try to gain some more information before he sent them on their way.

"If you'd like, you can wait in the back of my squad car while I call dispatch and fill out the report. I've got a blanket in the trunk that will help keep you warm."

Her eyes widened. "A police report?"

"A crash report is procedure, ma'am. It will give you something to send to your insurance company stating that the accident was caused by road conditions."

"Oh!" The visible relief he saw on her face made him wonder what her story was. Either she was so squeaky clean that she had never been in trouble a moment of her life, or she was hiding something. He wasn't going to have a repeat of what happened when he worked in Flint. If she was hiding something, he was going to find out what it was, and soon.

She stepped back to her car and grabbed her purse and a bigger bag. After looking in the direction of the billboard, she helped the boy out of the car, then took him by the hand and followed Max to his.

Chapter 3

AVA WAS GRATEFUL FOR the blanket and wrapped it around herself before sliding into the back of the squad car and letting Oliver climb onto her lap. She wondered how many other non-criminals had the pleasure of being seated back there and tried not to think about whether it was ever disinfected. It looked clean enough, but one never knew.

Oliver squirmed to look at the equipment in the front seat. He whispered, "Cool," a few times as he caught glimpses of each item on the dash. "Mom, can you take a picture? I want to draw this later."

"I don't think we're allowed to do that, sweetie. Take a picture with your eyes, okay?"

"Okay." He squinted as if trying to capture a mental picture. His fascination with the equipment in the squad car was enough of a distraction that she was able to feel around his head and arms to make sure he wasn't injured.

The officer—Officer Brody, according to his name tag—quickly typed away on his laptop after calling dispatch and asking them to call a tow truck, seemingly oblivious to the awe he was inspiring in her son. She glanced out the window, wondering what kind of service station would be in the small town and hoping it was both good and not very busy. The Sullivan and Son Realty billboard that had distracted her before taunted her from high above. She shivered again as she studied Jack Sullivan's face.

When Officer Brody looked up, their gazes met in the rearview mirror. His deep brown eyes matched his close-cropped hair and conveyed a world-weariness she could relate to. "Is there someone you can call, or can I drop you somewhere, ma'am?"

"No, we're from out of town." *Duh.* "Well, you know that. I'm Ava by the way, and this is Oliver."

"I'm Max. It looks like I have a few minutes, so if you'd like, I can drop you somewhere so you can at least get a warm cup of coffee while you wait."

Something warm sounded great. A cold walk back to the repair place did not. "Thank you, but we'll wait in the auto repair lobby."

He laughed. "It's not that kind of auto repair. There's no seating inside unless you count the crates of parts, but there's a diner down the street. They make a good cup of coffee and hot chocolate there, and it will be warmer than standing outside."

Oliver perked up at the mention of hot chocolate, and the officer winked at him in the rearview mirror.

"Okay, thank you." What was she going to do? She bowed her head. *Please, Lord, let the mechanic be able to fix my car quickly.*

As if in answer to prayer, the tow truck pulled up next to the squad car. The window lowered and the man inside smiled broadly at Officer Brody. "Hi again, Max."

"Afternoon, Al. What's this, number three for the day?" He gestured to the back seat with his thumb. "This is Ava."

Al tipped his hat in her direction. "Hi, Ava."

"When you get her car to Woody's, can you tell him I'm dropping them at the Bay Shore Diner? He's got her number."

Without further conversation, Al closed his window and angled his truck to get to her car.

As soon as they got back on the main road, the radio squawked with a report of a fender bender on Evergreen. Officer Brody responded, "Be right there." He met her eyes again in the rearview mirror. "Duty calls."

"We appreciate the ride, don't we, Oliver?" She nudged him to remind him of his manners.

"Thank you, officer. I always wanted to ride in a police car!"

Officer Brody met her gaze and smiled. "Just as long as you're riding in a police car as a good boy, Oliver."

"I'm usually a good boy, right Mom?"

"That's right. Usually." She kissed the top of his head, thankful that he hadn't been hurt in the accident.

The Bay Shore Diner was apparently on Officer Brody's way, so he dropped them off there with a wave and a salute to Oliver.

Oliver grinned from ear to ear. "This is the best day ever. I can't wait to tell my friends that I got to ride in a real police car." Always an optimist, Oliver had apparently forgotten about the accident that led to his *so cool* ride in the police car.

She shook off the humiliation of being let out of the back of a police cruiser and shuffled into the diner, keeping her head low and directing Oliver to the last booth in the back. She pretended to study the menu as she cursed the curiosity that had brought her to this town.

What was she really doing here, anyway? It wasn't like she was going to walk up to Jack Sullivan and drop the bombshell that he had a child.

Within minutes Oliver had his hot chocolate and she had a hot tea. They both held their cups to warm their fingers, and Oliver reminisced about every detail of his time in the squad car. Ava handed him his notepad and crayons so he could draw a few sketches of his adventure while they waited for their chili cheese fries.

Oliver's eyes grew wide when the waitress delivered their decadent snack. "We get to eat these? *And* hot chocolate?"

"Every once in a while we should have treats like hot chocolate and chili cheese fries, don't you think?"

He answered by lifting a fry and losing half of its topping before getting it to his mouth. "Yes!"

She and Oliver usually ate healthy, but the stress of the day warranted a dangerous meal with no guilt. After a brief conversation with Woody, she texted Sarita, relaying the unfortunate events that had happened since they ended their call an hour ago. Through it all, Oliver chattered about the cool police car, the cool police officer, and the super cool chili cheese fries. She really needed to work on expanding his vocabulary.

Less than ninety minutes had passed when Oliver grinned and waved at someone behind her. She looked up to see Officer Brody approaching their booth. His was the only familiar face in town— apart from the one on the billboard—and she was surprisingly grateful to see him.

He pointed at the mess on Oliver's plate. "You got chili cheese fries, champ? You must have a very nice mom."

Oliver's grin held remnants of both the cheese fries and the whipped cream from the hot chocolate. Ava smiled up at the man. "Checking up on us, officer?"

He chuckled and indicated the clothing he had in his hand. "I brought you some things from our Lost and Found at the station in case they might help. I don't want to have to respond to a call about any Floridians freezing during their visit."

Police station clothes? She wasn't in a position to decline anything that would keep them warm, so she accepted them. "I guess it's true what they say about small town hospitality, huh?"

"We aim to please." When she took the pile from his extended hand, he gestured toward an empty chair at a nearby table. "May I join you?"

Oliver looked like he had just won the lottery. "Yes!"

"Sure." Her response was less enthusiastic than Oliver's, but she tried to sound friendly.

Officer Brody signaled to the waitress, telling her in diner sign language that he would like a cup of coffee. "So, what brings you all the way from Florida without coats or gloves?"

She glanced around the room before speaking and, not seeing either of the faces from the billboard, answered as carefully as she could without lying. "I'm on a research trip, and we're turning it into an adventure. Aren't we, sweetie?"

Oliver bobbed his head up and down and raised a fry like a sword. "An adventure!"

"An adventure, huh?" The officer nodded in thanks to the waitress and took a sip of coffee as he studied her. "What kind of research?"

As if God was handing out answers to prayer like candy, her phone buzzed. Signaling apologies to her overly-curious companion, she answered. "Hi Woody."

"Afternoon, ma'am. This is going to take longer than I thought. Your accident damaged the wheel bearing and the suspension, but I won't know how bad the damage is until I can get it apart. I'll try to get to it tomorrow, but I've got a lot of cars in here with the roads as bad as they are."

She closed her eyes and sighed. "Okay, thank you. I'll wait to hear from you then." She ended the call and set her phone on the table.

Officer Brody looked up from the drawing of the police car Oliver had been showing him. "Problem?"

"It looks like it will be a while."

He frowned. "Sorry." After glancing at his watch, he looked back up at her. "My shift ends in about an hour. Can I drop you somewhere?"

Oliver almost jumped out of his seat. "Can we ride in the police car again?"

She shook her head and silenced Oliver with a look. "I'm sure we've taken up too much time out of your day already, Officer Brody."

"Max."

"Okay, Max. You don't need to shuttle us around town. Plus, we're staying on the other side of Lakes End." She hoped that would seem like far away in a rural area like this and that he would drop it. She would find a way to the hotel somehow.

Hanging out with a cop did not sound like the best way to spend her evening, even if he was especially friendly, helpful, and kind to her son. And cute. She winced. What was she, thirteen? *Cute? Really?*

He smiled, which made him even cuter. "It's not a problem at all. I live in Lakes End."

Of course you do.

"Cool!"

She barely stopped Oliver's hot cocoa from spilling all over him when he reached to high-five his new best friend and hero.

Inwardly Ava groaned. It was going to be a long afternoon.

Chapter 4

MAX DROPPED THE SQUAD car off at the station and changed into his civilian clothes. His dog was a retired K9, so unless Max was taking him out on a search and rescue or for a day at the station, he didn't wear his uniform or take a cruiser home. It was confusing for the dog, and he got depressed if he saw Max leave in uniform without him. Max nodded at Wyatt Henry on his way out the door.

Wyatt raised an eyebrow. "Got a date tonight?"

"Just a routine offer to drive someone home."

"The grin on your face suggests otherwise." Wyatt snickered when he looked at the ladies' scarf Max clutched in his hand. "Picking through the Lost and Found for a gift is a little beneath you, don't you think?"

Max waved at him as he frowned and strutted away. "Funny guy! Not a date!"

Not a date. It wasn't. She was a stranger from out of town who had a traumatic experience and needed a ride. Okay, *traumatic* was a little much for a minor motor vehicle accident, but she was shaken up and he was just being hospitable. Plus, there was a child to consider. He wasn't about to have her scrounge for a ride when she had a child to protect.

If he were honest, her nervousness was what made him blurt out the offer to drive her to the hotel more than their stranding or those incredible green eyes. He didn't take unnecessary risks with his town. Not anymore.

When he walked back into the diner, they were still seated in the back. Oliver was working on a drawing and Ava was nursing what was left of her tea. She was sitting in the same position as she had been earlier. If Max were trying to hide from someone, that was exactly where and how he would sit.

"Ready to go?"

She jumped at his voice. "We're ready, as long as you're sure."

He offered the scarf. "Found something else to help you keep warm."

"Thank you." She directed Oliver to put away his crayons and rose slowly from the booth, scanning the room with her eyes.

When Max gestured for her to lead the way out of the restaurant, she did so but took her time putting the scarf on and kept her face angled away from the other customers. He scanned the room himself to see if anyone was watching them. All he saw was a room full of mostly familiar faces focused on the food and company in front of them. Something didn't add up.

They walked quickly to Max's SUV, bracing against the frigid wind. "You have two cars?" Oliver's eyes were wide.

"I just have this one. The one you rode in earlier belongs to the police department. If it's okay with your mom, I'll let you sit in the front seat of the cruiser sometime."

Oliver jumped into the back seat as soon as Ava positioned his booster seat. "Mom, can I go in the police car again?"

"We'll see, sweetie."

Something was definitely going on with the woman.

Max whispered as he got in the car, "Sorry about that. I didn't mean to overstep by offering."

"It's fine. We're just not staying in town for too long."

Until they left or he was satisfied with what was going on with her, he planned to keep an eye on her. It didn't seem that the boy was in any danger, but Max would rather be safe than sorry.

"Thanks again for the ride." She rubbed her hands together in front of the vent as they made their way up the hill that led out of Hideaway. "And for the warm clothes. I'll return them as soon as I can go shopping."

"Don't worry about it. They were in the Lost and Found."

"Still . . ." She shrugged and nervously looked around the car. "Did you grow up here?"

Noting her abrupt change of topic but hoping she would be more likely to open up if he acted relaxed, he answered. "My grandparents had a place in Lakes End, so I spent most of the summer here. I moved here permanently five years ago when my grandpa needed help after a heart attack. How about you? Ever been to Michigan before?" He didn't have much time to pump her for information during the short ride, so he needed to keep her talking. With Oliver entertained watching the huge trees that lined the road, it seemed like the perfect time.

"No, this is the first time I've been north of Tennessee. My mom is from here though—well, from Michigan." Ava seemed to be focusing awfully hard at something outside the car window herself. That, or she was avoiding him.

"So, you're a hometown girl once removed."

"Something like that." She finally turned her head in his direction. "That's nice of you to help your grandpa out."

"It's good to have the time with him." He wasn't about to get into the other reasons he had for moving to Summit County. It was her reason for being there that he was interested in discussing, not his. "I hope the car problem doesn't slow down your research."

She flinched and looked back out the window. "No . . . I've got time."

"How long are you here for, anyway?"

"I'm not sure." She glanced at Oliver. "We don't have a home to go back to yet."

Oliver piped up from the back seat. "Hurricane Yolanda broke ours, right, Mom? Our shop too."

Ouch. "Sorry to hear that. Destroyed them?"

She shook her head. "Not quite, but almost. Our apartment and my shop—"

"Our shop."

She shot a grin back at Oliver. "*Our* shop and home are in a multi-use building, so when Yolanda hit, she took them both out. The landlord and the insurance company are arguing over what will happen with it right now. The insurance company wants it torn down, but it's in a historic area north of Miami. My landlord wants to preserve what little history is left there."

"What about you? Who do you hope wins?"

"History." There was something sad in her voice when she said the word.

"Is that what you're in Michigan looking for? History?"

She looked at him for a long moment, her eyes clouding over. "In a manner of speaking." She looked ahead on the road and pointed. "That's the hotel."

Did he hear relief in her voice? He didn't have enough information yet. Her vague answers only served to raise more questions in his mind.

"Are you hungry? Without a car, you're going to have a hard time finding dinner."

She lifted the lost-and-found sweater he had given her, revealing a takeout bag in her hand. "I ordered sandwiches and salad for us to eat later."

He scrambled for a reason to extend his time with them without alerting her to his suspicions as he pulled in front of the hotel. "Tomorrow is my day off, and I need to go into Hideaway. Would you like a ride to Woody's?"

Oliver answered from the back seat. "Yes, please."

She shook her head. "It's not necessary."

He winked at Oliver and smirked at her. "I'll pick you up at noon."

Chapter 5

AVA WAS THANKFUL WHEN Oliver fell asleep shortly after dinner. She flopped onto her own bed and stared at the ceiling, willing her thoughts to stop. Being around a cop and dodging questions was exhausting. So was being in a town and wondering if she had seen the man she'd come for.

Who was she kidding? One look at that billboard and she had known she'd found him. *Sullivan and Son Realty. So much for Pre-Law.* Was the rest of the limited information she had about Jack accurate?

Her phone buzzed. Seeing that it was Sarita, she answered with a laugh. "Enrique and the kids are going to hate me if you spend all your time talking to me and neglecting them."

"They're watching *Star Wars* again. Believe me, they didn't notice I left the room. So?"

"So, my car is still in the shop and I'm wearing lost-and-found clothes that I keep telling myself didn't come from a dead body." She shuddered at the thought. "I'm hoping that a bath and a good night's sleep will make me stop regretting this trip."

"Back up. What was that about a dead body?"

"My cold weather fashion is courtesy of the police department's Lost and Found box. I'm going shopping tomorrow for something not previously owned."

It took a minute for the laughter on the other end of the phone to stop. "You don't even like resale stores, but you went shopping at the police station?"

"No, the cop who saw the accident brought clothes to us while we were spending the afternoon at the diner devouring chili cheese fries." It did sound pretty absurd.

"Wow, what a nice cop."

"He's Oliver's new hero. He's been great with him." She smiled at the man's kind gestures, trying not to picture his strong jaw or the way his eyes wrinkled when he smiled. "It's a friendly town from what I can see."

"Oh? Tell me more about the friendly cop who took a shine to your son." The excitement was evident in her friend's voice.

She straightened up to a sitting position. "No. Don't start with that. You know how I am around cops, and he was asking questions about why we're here. We're not going to become besties or anything. He was just nice."

"You know, you could baby step with him too."

"What are you talking about?" As if she didn't know. Sarita had been urging her to get back into the dating arena for the last two years.

"Since you always get nervous around authority figures, you could practice acting relaxed around the nice-and-hopefully-single cop who is great with your son. Two birds with one stone, you know?"

Ava let out a guffaw. "Have you been sniffing the air around the pot shop? I don't want to *practice* anything or answer any questions from a nosy local, and I'm not here looking for a boyfriend. Or for Oliver to get attached to someone."

"I'm just saying, a little fun and romance could take away from some of the stress of your trip."

"No thanks. I'm going to let you go so I can get a bath and go to bed."

"Okay, fine—wait, how are you going to get your car?"

"Umm . . ." She twisted her ring. "The cop is driving us to town tomorrow."

"Oh, we're definitely going to be talking more about that! Good night."

She turned her phone off and plugged it in. She needed peace and quiet so she could figure out what to talk about on the ride to Hideaway tomorrow. The man asked too many questions, and she hated lying.

The bath was relaxing, but not enough to make her sleep through the night. Her dreams were invaded by the snow, the hill, the feeling of sliding down the embankment, and the smiling face from the billboard.

Woody called at eleven the next morning to tell her he didn't have the part for the car yet, but he hoped he would have it and the car would be done by four when he closed the shop for the day—as well as the weekend. It had never occurred to her that the auto shop wouldn't be open seven days. She hadn't even realized it was Friday until Woody told her. This trip was doing a number on her mind.

Please let the car be done today, Lord. What was she going to do if she had to wait until Monday to pick it up? The sooner she could get what she came for, the sooner she could go back home and get on with her life. Of course, in order to get what she had come so far for, she needed to figure out what that really was.

As promised, Officer Brody was waiting in front of the hotel at noon. "Taxi, at your service." Just like when he drove them home last night, he was much less intimidating in his sweater and jeans than in the uniform he wore when they first met. He was also even more attractive, but she tried not to notice. *Not here for a boyfriend.*

"Thank you again for this. My car isn't ready yet, but I was thinking that if you dropped us off someplace where we can buy some clothes and decent boots, we can walk to Woody's when we're done."

"Have you eaten lunch yet?"

Oliver climbed into his seat. "I'm hungry."

"We had meal bars an hour ago." Her traitorous stomach growled its displeasure at the sorry excuse for a morning snack.

"Those don't count. How would you like to stop at my favorite place in Lakes End? My treat."

Oliver recovered from his disappointment at not riding in the police car at the mention of food. "Yes, please."

Both of them looked at her, waiting for an answer.

Her heart raced. More conversation meant more hiding. In her entire thirty-nine years, eleven months, and ten days, she had never skirted the truth as much as she had in the last twenty-four hours.

"I really don't want to be a bother."

When he smiled at her, she noticed that he had a tiny dimple. "We're all hungry and we all have time. Right?"

No arguing that. "How can I say no?"

Chapter 6

WHEN MAX HELD THE door to the Rock Creek Tavern for Ava and Oliver, she did the same quick scan of the room that he had seen her do yesterday. The place was about half full, typical for this time of year. Next weekend it would be packed with people in town for Thanksgiving, but today there was plenty of seating.

She looked relieved after searching the room and even more so when they were ushered toward a booth in the back.

He gestured for her to sit first so she could choose where she felt comfortable. Not surprisingly, she chose the one that faced away from other patrons. He pretended not to notice and kept his tone casual. "It's warmer back here, so it should be better suited to easily-frozen Floridians."

She smiled. She was even prettier when she put down her guard. "Perfect. We put on as many clothes as we could reasonably layer this morning."

"I can't move in all these." Oliver pulled up his sweatshirt to reveal another one plus a shirt underneath.

Ava helped him take off the top layer. "Better?"

"Better." He moved his arms around, demonstrating his newfound freedom.

When she pulled the pad and crayons from his tote bag and set them in front of him, he immediately started drawing a snowy scene with Christmas trees and a snowman. She looked back up at Max. "We'll go shopping today and return these clothes to the station."

"It's no problem, really."

"Well, someone might need them." She held her hand up between them, blocking her face, and leaned forward so she could whisper. "Don't tell me if they came from a dead body until after I've returned them. Please."

He almost choked on the water he had just sipped.

She held up a finger, just the way his mother used to warn him. "Tell me later." She picked up the menu and started looking it over.

Once he stopped coughing, he deadpanned, "Lost and Found is different from the evidence room."

Her laugh caught him off guard. "That's a relief. What do you recommend?"

"Everything is great here. This time of year, I usually add a cup of soup. Good for keeping you warm."

Nodding, she closed the menu. "I think we'll each have a cup of the chicken noodle and a salad."

"Good call. How's your research going?"

Now it was her turn to choke on a drink. "Uh—fine, I guess."

"Can I help?" The sadness in her eyes told him whatever she was in town for was deeply important to her. The sudden fidgeting with Oliver's water told him she didn't like his questions. Suspicion and compassion warred within him as he waited to see if she would answer.

She kept her eyes down, as if carefully choosing her words. "Thank you, but the research is more of a personal nature. It's not really anything anyone can help with." Pulling her phone from her purse, she glanced up at him. "Do you mind if I leave this out in case Woody calls?"

"Sure." He redirected his attention toward her son. "That's a great picture, Oliver. How old are you?"

The boy held up four fingers. "Four—I mean five." He stared at his thumb as if it didn't belong with the other digits. Max's suspicion took note.

Ava stroked his hair and smiled. "He had a birthday less than a month ago, so he's still getting used to the new number."

His inner cynic wondered.

"Auntie Sarita had a party for me. We had a piñata and it was full of candy and I bursted it open!" Judging by the way his eyes danced, the story was legit.

"He loved hitting the piñata with his new baseball bat."

"That sounds like a good birthday party." Maybe if he could keep him talking for a minute, he would stay under Ava's radar long enough to find something out. He couldn't be too careful with his town. "Do you go to school?"

"I did, but Yolanda broke my school too." He pushed his lip out in a pout. "Mommy makes me do homework every morning so I'm ready for big school next year."

"It's important to be ready before you go to big school." He nodded toward the picture. "You like drawing, huh?"

"I love it!" The boy held up his snowman drawing. "This is a snow baseball."

Not a snowman, then. "That's a great drawing."

Ava nodded toward the drawing and gave him a knowing look. "Have you ever seen a snow baseball, Officer Brody?"

"That is my first." She seemed more relaxed, so he snuck in a question for her. "So, how long do you plan to stay in town?"

Oliver paused his drawing and looked at her. "I want to stay here and ride in the police car again. Can we, Mom?" She was about to answer when the waitress came to take their orders. *Again with the relieved look.* What was she hiding?

After giving their orders, he changed course. Direct questions only seemed to make her jumpy.

"When did Woody say the car would be ready?"

She cupped the hot tea the waitress delivered. "He hopes by four. Speaking of that, would you mind dropping us off at a clothing store? We can walk to the auto shop from there."

The woman was too much. "Did you notice the gray sky out there? It's going to be snowing again soon. I can drop you off, run my errands, and take you back to Woody's."

When she started to protest, he put his hand up. "It's no trouble."

She sighed. "If you're sure."

"I'm sure." *I'm also sure I'm going to learn your secrets.*

As they sat and talked about safe topics—Oliver's drawing and love for green, the weather, the scenic places around Summit County, the car—she seemed to relax. Even though his gut said she was not likely to be a threat to his community, something was going on.

He wanted to know more about her. What he had gathered so far was that she had never been in any kind of trouble, hated to be a burden to people, took excellent care of her son, had secrets, and feared something in his town. Maybe it wasn't his town that needed the protecting, but Ava and Oliver.

Chapter 7

BY THE TIME MAX—HE had threatened arrest if she continued to use his last name—dropped them off by some clothing stores on Main Street, Ava was feeling more comfortable with him. He had finally given up his interrogation of her and started acting more like a regular person than a cop. She had soon found that when they talked about normal subjects, he was interesting, funny, and great with Oliver.

It was too bad she hadn't met anyone like him at home. If the circumstances were different, he was someone she would have liked to have gotten to know better.

Following his suggestion, Ava and Oliver started their shopping spree in a children's store, then went two doors down to the women's store where he said he would pick them up. The bell jingled over the door when they walked in.

An older woman greeted them quickly. "Welcome to Up North Clothing and Treasures. Let me know if you need any help."

Ava returned her smile. "Thank you, we will."

"Mom needs some clothes to go out in the snow."

Ava chuckled at Oliver's extroverted nature. The boy would never lack for friends.

The woman approached them and leaned down to Oliver's eye level. "Did you get some clothes too?"

Oliver spun around to show off his new green coat and mittens. "I'm going to build a snow baseball."

"A snow baseball, you say? I've never seen such a thing."

Oliver didn't miss a beat. "I'll draw one for you."

"You will? I would love to see one."

"I draw pictures for people at our shop, so I can draw it real fast." He held up his bag of art supplies.

"I have a little table back there that would be just the right size for you." She turned to Ava. "Would you like me to set your bags over by the register for you?"

She handed the bags to the woman. "That would be wonderful. Thank you." *Smart woman, offering to free my hands up for shopping. I could learn a thing or two here.* "I'm Ava and this is Oliver."

"It's a pleasure to meet you, Ava and Oliver. I'm Colette, and I own the store." The woman looked to be well into her seventies, but the way she dressed and the glint in her eye suggested she was as spry as someone half her age. She had wavy white hair that was cut in a spiky, young style and a flowing dress that looked like something she could wear for just about any occasion with the proper accessories. She radiated warmth, and Ava was as instantly drawn to her as she was to her store.

"You have a great place here."

Colette beamed like a proud parent. "Thank you. I do love it. How about if I show your young artist to the coffee table while you look around?"

Ava noted the small sitting area in the back corner of the store. *Brilliant.* "That's perfect. Thank you."

"Come along, Oliver. I can't wait to see what a snow baseball looks like."

Ava watched them go. It would be good for Oliver to have a little taste of home. Her greatest achievement as a parent had been to convince Oliver that going to work with her was an adventure and that her shop was as much his as it was hers. His drawings were famous among her regulars, so it was no stretch of the truth to say that the shop's success was bolstered by him.

She quickly found some sweaters to try on and decided to buy two of them. The style and quality were exquisite, and she made a mental note to see if the company made clothing more fitting for Miami's climate. There would be plenty of restocking to be done when she reopened her shop. *If* she could reopen it.

When she exited the fitting room with her chosen purchases in one arm and the folded rejects in the other, Oliver was telling Colette about his regular artwork customers. The woman took both stacks of sweaters and tilted her head toward the middle of the store. "We have some others in these styles if you like."

"Oh, thank you. We're only in town for a short visit, so I think these two should be enough." She glanced down at the display in front of her. "I will take that scarf. It will go with both sweaters and keep my neck from frostbite." She had already found a cute coat on the clearance rack. Next stop, boots.

When she picked up a pair with a nice heel that caught her eye, Colette appeared at her side. "Are you looking for something for show or to walk around in without breaking your neck?"

She chuckled sheepishly. "A little of both, maybe?"

Colette pulled the boot out of her hand and walked to the end of the row. The one she picked up had a much shorter heel but had a cute little strap near the ankle. "This one will show off those great legs of yours and keep you off the crutches." Ava turned the boot over and checked the price.

With a smile, Colette pulled the matching boot from its box and handed it to her. "I'm more interested in safety and repeat business than in selling the most expensive shoe every time."

"I like you, Colette. You run your shop the way I run mine."

The woman chuckled. "Oliver has been telling me all about his special customers."

"A lot of my repeat business is thanks to his artwork. Customers love getting the chance for a picture." She slid the boots on and walked along the aisle in them. "These fit perfectly."

"They look great! And with that little bit of grip on the bottom you won't break anything when you walk on the sidewalk."

"If I planned to stay in town, I would definitely be a repeat customer here." The store reminded her so much of hers, even though it had different ratios of the types of merchandise. There was something for every style and every price range and was clearly set up to tempt visitors to stay awhile.

When she approached the counter to pay for her purchases, she looked with appreciation at the gift items and knickknacks displayed near it. "You've done a nice job with the impulse buy section."

Colette laughed. "Is that what you call it where you're from?"

"I don't know what the rest of Miami calls it, but it's what I call it. Thirty percent of my sales come from within ten feet of the cash register."

Looking around, Colette nodded. "I imagine it's about the same here. Yours is also a women's store?"

"No, more of a gift store. I've got a small clothing section, but the rest is jewelry, accessories, souvenirs, and home décor. I try to have a little bit of everything to please both the tourists and the locals."

She waved her hand toward the front of the store. "Just like you have here."

Colette was still ringing the items up when Ava asked, "Would it be okay if I used your changing room again? I would like to get out of these borrowed clothes and return them."

"Certainly. Do you have time for a cup of tea after you change? I'm due to sit down for a break and would love to talk shop some more with you and Oliver."

Ava looked outside. There was no sign of Max yet, and she was enjoying talking to the woman. "I would love that."

Ava felt much more comfortable in clothes that she had chosen and fit her curves properly. She and Colette sat in a pair of chairs in the sitting area with Oliver, sharing retail stories and laughing together while he drew more pictures. It felt good to laugh and talk with Colette. Despite outward appearances, she reminded Ava a bit of her mother.

Her mother's style couldn't be more opposite of Colette's. She had continued to wear her tailored suits and sleek updo with no hair out of place until shortly before she died. Still, she would have loved Colette and would have bonded with her as instantly as Ava had.

By the time Max walked in, Colette felt like an old friend. Ava was disappointed to have their visit come to a stop.

"Maxwell!" Colette jumped to her feet and hugged Max. "What a nice surprise. How's your granddad?"

"He's great. He told me to let you know he's happy to help out if you have extra pumpkin bread again." When Max winked at the woman, Ava found herself wishing she was on the receiving end of it.

Not here for a boyfriend.

Colette pulled him by the hand to where Ava stood. "Maxwell, I would like you to meet my new friends, Ava and Oliver."

He grinned at Ava, then Colette. "Actually, I'm their ride."

Why did she feel all warm inside when he said that? This was not part of her plan. She was supposed to sneak into town, get what she came for, and leave without anyone knowing she'd been there.

Chapter 8

MAX EYED AVA'S NEW look with appreciation. She was no less than stunning when she was relaxed and enjoying herself. She and Colette had obviously clicked, and she seemed to have let her guard fully down with the dear woman. If he didn't know better, he would think they had known each other for years.

She held up the clothes from the Lost and Found. "I'll have these laundered and return them to you as soon as I can."

"No!" He feigned horror. "They can't be washed before they go back into evidence!" Her laugh made his chest swell. Making a beautiful woman laugh did all kinds of good to a man's ego. At least this man.

Colette swiped him playfully on the arm. "You be nice to our out-of-town visitor, Maxwell."

Ava came to his defense. "He's been more than nice since we crashed into town—quite literally."

"Your grandma would be proud." The woman would know. She was one of his grandma's closest friends until the day she died six years ago and had always been good to him and his grandpa.

"He's going to take us back to the auto repair."

"Actually, I have an idea for a stop first, if you're up for it."

Oliver appeared at his side. "Is it a ride in the police car?"

Max chuckled. He was definitely going to need to make that happen before they left. "Sorry, champ. I'm not working today, so I don't have my squad car." He leaned down and whispered his plans into Oliver's ear, making the little boy giggle.

After saying their goodbyes to Colette, the threesome walked to Max's car.

"Ready for my idea?"

Ava gave him a sideways glance. "That depends. What is it?"

Oliver started giggling again. "It's a really, really good idea, Mom."

Max pulled out of the angled parking spot and drove toward the high school. The parking lot would be empty on a Saturday in November and perfect for a lesson. "Well as you know, I'm a public safety officer, and you are a danger to my public."

Her eyes widened. "Me? How?"

"Do you remember how we met?"

She arched a brow and crossed her arms in defense. "I'll have you know, *Officer Brody*, that was my first accident. I'm a very safe driver. Once my car is fixed, I won't be a danger anymore."

When she punctuated her sentence with a huff, he couldn't contain his laugh. "Your car didn't cause that accident. Your driving did."

"Did not!"

He snickered and exchanged a grin with Oliver as he pulled to the center of the ice-covered parking lot. Getting out, he walked to the passenger side and opened Ava's door. "Out of the car, please." He held his hand out to her. "Watch your step."

"I'm perfectly capable of—" She slipped on the slick pavement and grabbed his arms to stop the fall, which he didn't mind one bit. After righting herself, she scowled at the ground.

"You were saying?" He angled his arm for her to take it and ushered her to the driver's side door.

When he returned to the passenger seat, her face was ashen. "That was really my fault?"

His chest constricted. He hadn't meant to make her feel bad with his teasing. "Don't worry about it. You haven't had practice driving on winter roads. That's why we're here."

She eyed the parking lot warily. "I knew I should have stayed home."

"Ava, look at me."

When she turned to him, she looked terrified. It was obviously uncomfortable for her to be in such a vulnerable position.

"I'm here to help. Trust me, I've had accidents on slick roads and I know how to avoid them—or at least stack the odds in my favor." He put his hand on her arm. "Do you trust me to teach you?"

"It's okay, Mom. Officer Max is going to fix your driving."

She nodded and gave a nervous smile.

"Okay. Before we start, I want you to look around. We're nowhere near anything you could hit, so we're safe. Start driving like you would on Florida roads."

She gestured toward the back seat and Oliver. "But . . ."

"If it wasn't safe, I wouldn't have brought you here. Go ahead."

As expected, as soon as she pushed the gas pedal, the car started sliding. She gasped and hit the brake, which sent it into a spin.

Oliver squealed. "Cool!"

Max kept a calm and reassuring tone to his voice as he guided her. "Foot off the pedal . . . now slowly touch the brake . . . keep it light . . . good."

She followed his instructions to the letter and only slid a couple of times. When she brought the car to a stop, she put it back into Park and dropped her hands in her lap. "I never want to drive on ice again."

"You did great."

She looked at him like he didn't understand simple concepts. "I don't think that means what you think it means."

He laughed. "When you're learning something new, it's good to see why the old way doesn't work."

"I definitely see why the old way doesn't work." She was still staring at the steering wheel. "What am I supposed to do, though? And how am I going to get home?"

He suspected the fear in her eyes wasn't just about driving. "I promise, I'll make sure you know how to handle this. Ready to try again?"

"Yeah, let's do that again!"

"Officer Max was showing me what not to do, Oliver. I'm trying not to do that again."

"Aw, man!"

Max stifled his laugh at the little boy's enthusiasm. "Despite what your little adrenaline junkie says, try it again with less pressure on the pedal."

After taking a deep breath and squaring her shoulders, determination washed over her face. The woman was not afraid of a challenge.

"Tell me what to do."

"Okay, remember how when you used a light touch on the pedals, the car came under control?"

She nodded. "Yes."

"Okay, try it with the gas. And if you feel the tires slipping underneath you, ease up on it without hitting the brakes."

"Okay." She took a deep breath and closed her eyes.

He wondered if she was praying like he was in that moment.

This time when she started, the car moved in a straight line. She drove about twenty yards and slowly brought it to a stop.

"Good job, Mom."

"I did it!" Her face radiated pure joy.

"You did it. Want to try again?"

This time when she nodded, it was with vigor and excitement, not resignation. "What do I do for turns?"

"Slow well before you need to turn, and you'll do fine. You've got this."

"I've got this."

She was a fascinating woman. In the span of ten minutes, he'd seen her as vulnerable as a baby chick, then terrified, and finally determined. He got the feeling she was a woman who always landed on her feet.

When her phone buzzed, she carefully brought the car to a stop and put it in Park before answering.

"Was that for my benefit?"

Her brows furrowed like she had no idea what he was talking about. His mind flashed to her clean driving record. Maybe it was just how she operated—always careful, always following the rules. No wonder she was horrified when he said her driving caused the accident.

Her face fell when Woody said something. "Okay . . . and you're not open tomorrow or Sunday . . . Are you sure it will be there on Monday?"

He tried to give a sympathetic look, even though he was not at all disappointed by the idea of being their tour guide and chauffeur for a little longer. Knowing Woody would have the car for at least a few days, he was glad he only had to work one day over the weekend.

"The car isn't ready?"

She shook her head and the fear returned to her eyes. "Not until Monday at the earliest."

What was she so afraid of? His curiosity tried to get the better of him, but he didn't want her to clam up like she had earlier when he had asked direct questions. "I guess we have some more time to practice then."

Her eyes lit up in excitement, but then she shook her head. "It's okay. I'm sure you had other plans for today."

He realized how glad he was that he didn't when he looked down at the time on the dash. "I've got two hours before I need to be home to make dinner for my grandfather. The only thing I need to do before that is stop at the grocery store. Plenty of time for a few more practice rounds."

"Yes!" Oliver clapped his hands. "Let's spin again!"

Chapter 9

AVA WAS GETTING MORE confident in her winter driving skills —at least while they were still in the high school parking lot. To Oliver's disappointment, she managed to keep the car under control through a few more stops and turns. She balked when Max suggested they move to a side street, but he convinced her that she should practice as much as possible with a teacher at her side.

He was a great teacher. He told her exactly how to do things and was patient when it took time for her to catch on. When they got a block away from the road she'd had her accident on, she pulled to the side and stopped the car.

As if he knew what she was thinking, he said, "You can do this, and it's no trouble. Come on, we've got a few minutes and we'll end at the store."

The store. Please, Lord, let him mean a store that's not in Hideaway. It's exhausting trying to be invisible in Jack Sullivan's town.

She hadn't realized Max was staring at her. "What is it?"

She waved a hand in the air. "Just nervous about driving on main roads in someone else's car."

He gestured to turn right. "You have nothing to be nervous about. You're a good driver, the car is insured, and you have an excellent teacher." His wink and playful smile just about put her over the edge.

The road wasn't covered in ice like the parking lot had been, so it was much easier to navigate. He led her down a tree-lined street that looked like something out of a movie. The leaves had fallen from the trees, and a light coat of snow covered everything from the trees and old houses to the street. There was a quietness there that she had never experienced. It was as if they had just driven into a Christmas card.

Not wanting to break up the peacefulness of the scene, she whispered, "Wow, I see what I missed out on growing up in a place that doesn't have seasons. It's beautiful." Even Oliver was quiet as he looked out the window.

Max sighed. "Oh, man. You never got to experience any of this, did you? I'm sorry for your loss."

She chuckled. "Somehow I've managed. This is amazing, though."

His eyes grew wide. "You've never made a snowman then, have you?"

"A snowman? No, but I've seen them on TV."

His deep laugh filled the car. "That's not the same. Suddenly it makes sense that your son draws baseballs instead of snowmen."

Oliver's wiggling caught her attention in the rearview mirror. "I want to make a snowman."

When they passed an old white church, Ava slowed the car to a crawl to gaze in wonder at it. Three women and two men were filing in with boxes overflowing with what looked like the makings of a Thanksgiving dinner, all smiling and chatting. "Wow."

Max waved at them. "They must be bringing supplies for Sunday."

"They eat a meal at the church service?"

He smiled. "No, there are a few churches that make Thanksgiving baskets for needy families in the area. It's First Community's turn to host the packaging this year."

"Oh, that's wonderful. Our church in Florida does that, but I've always been working when they've done the packaging."

"Our church in Lakes End is part of it, so we'll be here to help pack boxes Sunday after the service. Would you like to join us for church and boxing up the dinners?"

Going to a quaint little church and doing something to help someone sounded too good to pass up. "I would love to. What do you think, Ollie?"

"Yeah!"

Max gasped and clutched his chest. "Really? I didn't have to beg you or threaten to arrest you or convince you that it would be no trouble to pick you up?"

She playfully rolled her eyes at him. "It would feel good to serve someone. Do we get to go to the church service too?"

"Sorry, my grandfather never misses the service at our church. His grandfather helped to build it, so he feels very loyal to it. Are you up for going to the service there and then coming here?"

The idea of two quaint churches in one day sounded fabulous. "That sounds perfect."

"You have a grandpa, Officer Max?"

Max turned in his seat to face Oliver. "I do, and he was very impressed with the tree picture you made for me. We put it on our refrigerator as soon as I brought it home."

"Cool. I don't have a grandpa. I don't have a dad either."

Ava heard the tone that had crept into Oliver's voice at his matter-of-fact proclamation. She had known the day would come when he would realize that his family was different, just like she had as a little girl. "Ollie, maybe you could make a special picture for Officer Max's grandpa. I'll bet he would like that."

"Okay! Does he like baseball?"

Max grinned. "Are you kidding? He loves it!"

They continued to the end of the street, where he directed her to turn left. She was feeling more confident after not sliding once, and she did what she was told.

When his navigation led them to Lake Michigan, she felt like she was looking at a piece of home. "It looks just like the ocean—apart from the snow on the beach, of course."

"Can we get out, Mom?"

Without asking if Max minded, she parked the car. Stepping out, she closed her eyes and took a deep breath. It was strange to breathe in the crisp air that didn't have a hint of salt, but she let its coolness fill her lungs. Oliver ran toward the snow as soon as Max let him out of the back seat.

When she opened her eyes, Max was next to her, looking at her with a bemused smile.

Gesturing to their surroundings, she said, "This is beautiful."

He held her gaze, making her heart skip a beat or two, before turning toward the lake. "Yes, it is."

Ava savored the moment until she reminded herself that she was playing with fire. There was no future in this charming town or with this wonderful man. Pretending otherwise was foolish.

"Oliver, let's go! We need to go to the store so Officer Max can get home."

Max nudged her and spoke quietly. "We have some time. The store is on the way."

Oliver dragged his feet in the snow as he made his way toward them. "Can't I play in the snow for a few minutes?"

"We'll play in the snow when we get back to the hotel, I promise." She avoided Max's questioning expression as she herded Oliver toward the car. "We don't want to make Officer Max late, and we need to think about what we're going to get at the store for our special picnics in the room this weekend."

"Can I get cereal?"

She thanked God for her easily-redirected child. "We'll pick out something that's not too unhealthy but that's fun, okay?"

With Max back in the driver's seat, Ava relaxed.

Oliver called from the back seat, "Is Mom's driving fixed, Officer Max?"

He looked at her, then at Oliver. "Not yet, champ."

"Are we gonna have to stay in Michigan until the snow melts?"

Max laughed and probably missed her wince. "I would be happy to give her another lesson, Oliver. She'll be fine."

She was already regretting coming to Jack's town, and the thought of being trapped here for the winter was not a good one. "Did you hear that? I'll be able to drive us home just fine."

"Can we spin again when we have the next lesson?"

She reached back and tickled her daredevil son's leg. "The point of the lessons is to not spin, mister."

Max drove past the grocery store in Hideaway and continued up the hill that led out of town. "Did we accidentally use up your shopping time?" She needed groceries if she and Oliver were going to be stuck in the hotel without a car for the weekend, so she hoped he was still planning to stop somewhere.

"We do have more than one grocery store in Summit County. Only one stoplight, but plenty of grocery stores." Max's smile once again made her wish she'd met him under different circumstances. Despite his occasional interrogations, he was fun and easy to be around.

"Just making sure. Now that we're going to be stranded at the hotel without my car all weekend, I need the shopping trip too."

"You're only stranded until Sunday morning, remember? I'll be by early to pick you up for church."

His smile warmed her and made her want things she couldn't have. Between Max and Colette, this trip was stirring up too many things in her. She shook off the thought and pulled up her grocery list app.

Chapter 10

MAX DIDN'T TASTE A thing as he finished off his sandwich. His mind was far from the late meal and the havoc created by the few inches of snow that had fallen during their shift.

"I never thought I would wish for time to sit at my desk and fill out reports." Wyatt's voice pulled him out of his daze.

"Yeah." The last thing Max was in the mood for was small talk, but he went along with it.

"I ordered those elephants the other day. They'll be a good replacement for the squad cars."

"Mm-hm—" *What?* Max shot him a look. "What are you blabbering on about?"

The man laughed as he slowly chewed his food. "You want to tell me what's going on?" Wyatt's voice held more gentle command than question.

"No." Max didn't want to think about it, let alone talk about it. It was bad enough that old memories filled his dreams and made sleep fleeting last night.

Wyatt nudged his chair. "Do it anyway."

"You're awful bossy today."

"I'm told that's part of my charm."

Max laughed. "That's not a compliment."

"Potato, po-tah-to."

Their banter and the routine they had when they worked together made it easier to work weekends. They had their own system for handling crises and splitting up tasks, and it worked well. Still, he didn't feel like getting into it. Maybe he should find some paperwork himself.

"You've been in your head today." Despite his earlier joking, Wyatt was scrutinizing him.

Max let out the sigh that had been building up. "You're right." He might as well get it out. Wyatt knew everything and was a trustworthy sounding board. "I've been getting reminders of Flint this week."

All traces of humor left his friend's eyes. "What brought that on?"

"The woman I told you about, the one with the son. She's hiding something."

"And it's setting off your spidey sense?"

Max shook his head. "No. That's just the thing." He pictured the fear he had seen in Ava's eyes at times. "She seems genuine in every way, but she's in town for something and won't say what it is. The way she acts sometimes sets off my alarm bells."

Wyatt studied him. "Are the alarm bells legit?"

"Something is definitely going on. She gets this fear in her eyes every now and then, and she hides her face in public. I took them to the grocery store yesterday, and she paused before turning into every aisle. But she's here for something that has her rattled." He scrubbed his face with his hands. "I don't know if the town needs protecting or if she does."

"And you're afraid you're missing some clue because you're attracted to her."

Max's head snapped up. "I didn't say that."

"You didn't have to."

"It wouldn't be the first time I missed important clues because of a woman."

Wyatt leaned back in his chair and crossed his arms. "What evidence do you have that she's dangerous?"

Max wiped his mouth and threw the napkin into the trash bin with more force than necessary. "Cecilia." He couldn't help but spit the word.

"Cecilia isn't evidence. She's a painful lesson and part of your distant past. Does this woman remind you of her?"

He shuddered. "Not at all." Cecilia wasn't fit to scrape gum from Ava's shoes.

"Then why the concern?"

"You know as well as I do." Max stood and began pacing the floor. "People almost died on my watch last time. I'm not letting it happen again."

"That was a long time ago. You were off your game then, and she was a master manipulator."

That she was. She saw a burned-out, jaded man ripe for the picking, and offered a no-frills good time. Or so he thought.

"What does your gut tell you?"

Max took a swig of his cold, stale coffee. "That Ava's good." She was more than good. Seeing her with her son provided all the proof he needed for that. "That she's tried to live a mistake-free life."

"What else?"

"That she's afraid." Max leaned on the back of his chair and sighed. "She needs something here, but it terrifies her. It doesn't make sense."

Wyatt slowly put his lunch containers away and stood. "So find out what it is, for your own peace of mind if nothing else. When are you going to see her again?"

"Tomorrow. They're coming to church with us, then helping with the Thanksgiving baskets at First Community."

"Sounds like opportunity."

Max nodded. "I need to be careful with questions, get past her guard. Act more like a cop than a man."

When Max started for the door of the break room, Wyatt stopped him. "I've been here long enough and had enough clout that if I didn't trust your instincts or abilities, we would never work a shift together. I've always requested shifts with you, even after you told me the whole story of what happened in Flint. That should tell you everything you need to know about what kind of cop I think you are."

"Thanks, man." Coming from Wyatt, that was a high compliment.

A call came through on the radio, and they both walked through the door and toward the patrol car. Wyatt paused before putting the car into gear. "What happened in Flint taught you a hard lesson, but it doesn't define you. It also doesn't mean you can't have feelings for a woman. What do you get when you pray about this?"

"That she's a good woman and needs help." *And I want to be the one to help her.*

"Sounds like you're acting like a cop *and* a man. You know what to do then."

Wyatt was right. This was nothing like last time. Ava was afraid of something and, if anything, he needed to step up his investigation. If she was in trouble, he was going to be there to protect her and Oliver. This time there would be no distractions, no mistakes, and no near misses.

Chapter 11

AVA WATCHED OLIVER WALK back and forth between the windows while they waited for Max in the hotel lobby. Spending all day yesterday playing in the snow on the lawn of the hotel had tired him out, but he woke up ready for more today. If he'd said he loved Michigan once, he'd said it a thousand times. She had to admit, she loved it too. No wonder her mom always missed it.

"When is Officer Max gonna get here?"

If she had a dollar for every time he talked about Max, she could retire. "He's not supposed to pick us up for a few minutes. He's not late, we're early."

"I wish he would be early too. I can't wait to show him the snow angels we made yesterday."

She looked at the snow falling and adjusted his hat over his ears. "I'm sorry, sweetie, but I think the snow already covered them up."

His lower lip had almost popped out when he broke into a grin. "I'll make a new one at the church!"

"That's a great idea—*after* the service. He'll be very impressed."

"Do you think he knows about snow angels?"

"I'm sure he does, but he'll love to see yours." She hoped she'd made the right decision when she had accepted the invitation to spend the day with Max and his grandfather. Oliver already worshipped Max, and he was going to be a sad little boy when their Michigan visit ended and they had to go home. He wouldn't be the only one.

He started jumping up and down. "There he is!"

Ava's heart jumped a little bit too. She took a deep breath. *He's a vacation friend, nothing more.*

Oliver grabbed her hand and pulled her toward the door. "Come on, let's go."

By the time they got to the car, Max was standing outside it with his hand stretched toward Oliver's booster seat. "Allow me." He took it and opened her door. "Get inside before you freeze."

It took him a couple of minutes, but he figured out the seat and helped Oliver get buckled in, all while listening to Oliver's stories of playing in the snow and the pool since they last saw him.

She needed those moments to get over his Sunday look. She hadn't been prepared to see him in a suit and dress coat. When he got into the seat next to her, she forced herself to look away. This was no time to allow herself to indulge her eyes or let feelings grow. "How was work? Busy Saturday?"

"You have no idea." He shook his head. "I lost count of the minor traffic accidents."

"I thought you said this weather was safe to drive in if you knew how." Were her lessons going to be enough to allow her to drive home safely?

"It is. The problem is that summer makes people forget how to drive in snow." He tipped his head in her direction. "Lucky for you, I remember."

She couldn't help but laugh. "Lucky for us."

"Officer Max, do you know what a snow angel is?"

He looked at Oliver in the rearview mirror. "I do. Do you?"

"Yeah! Mom and I made a bunch of them yesterday. I wanted to show you, but she said they're covered up now. Can I make a new one at your church?"

"You sure can. You should probably wait until after the service ends, though."

"That's what Mom said too."

He winked in her direction, sending her heart jumping again. "Smart mom."

Max's grandfather, Vernon, was at the church when they arrived. He was a greeter and seemed to know everyone there, but paid special attention to Oliver. "I've been looking forward to meeting the artist who created the drawing on my refrigerator."

"That's where Mom put them when we had a refrigerator too."

The man seemed to catch on immediately. "I hear Yolanda did some damage down your way."

Oliver nodded solemnly. "She broke everything."

"We're going to pick out replacements when we move back into our apartment." Ava rested her hands on his shoulders. "Our next refrigerator will have plenty of room for Oliver's art."

"That will be a fine-looking refrigerator, then." When a family walked through the door, he pointed toward the sanctuary. "I've saved you a special seat up front by me today. How does that sound?"

Oliver's shoulders straightened. "Good. I like to sit near the front too. That's where the people who listen sit."

Max turned to hide his snicker and held out his hand to Oliver. "Let's go get the seats warmed up, champ."

It took a while to get to the pew with so many people greeting Max. Seeing him with his grandfather and the others there did nothing to halt her growing feelings. It was obvious that he was well-liked and respected among the congregation. The way he filled out his suit was a pleasant, if dangerous, bonus.

As the pastor spoke about the vine and branches, Oliver drew them. Their discussions about church and the things he got out of it were one of her favorite things about Sundays. His childlike faith inspired her own.

Vernon recited the Scripture passage without a Bible or notes. The reminder that her strength came from Jesus, not herself, was exactly what she needed to hear. Abiding didn't come naturally to her after a lifetime of trying to perform and do everything asked and expected of her. *Please show me how to abide in You during this trip, Lord. You're the only One who can sustain me. Make our time in Michigan about Your will, not mine.*

Chapter 12

WHILE THEY DROVE FROM Lakes End Christian Church to First Community, Max listened as Gramps told Ava and Oliver all about growing up in the church his great-grandfather built. Gramps was a carpenter himself, so he went into detail about the expansion and repairs he had himself made over the years.

"Maxwell here knows how to swing a hammer, too."

Max grinned at the man who had taught him everything he knew. "Not as well as you, Gramps."

He shook his head. "Don't let him fool you, Ava. He got the carpentry gene. We'll have you for dinner and you can see the built-in bookcase he made for his grandma."

Ava and Oliver were clearly charmed by Gramps, and they seemed to hold onto his every word. Gramps was equally taken with them, judging by the extra sparkle in his eye as he told his stories. He didn't get many opportunities to regale pretty young women or precocious children with tales from days gone by, so he was taking full advantage of his platform.

Max dropped them off in front of the church, then parked the car down the street. When he walked into the busy dining room, Oliver was in the kids' craft corner and Ava and Gramps were sitting at a table with Colette, separating dinner rolls into bags. Ava seemed so relaxed as she laughed with the older folks—nothing like the woman who had been looking over her shoulder in the restaurants or dodging his questions.

He greeted Pastor Ray and other friends as he made his way to their table, shaking hands and receiving hugs from the people who had welcomed him to their community so quickly after his arrival. Sometimes it was hard to believe it had only been five years.

Once seated, he donned his gloves and got to work. It took less than two hours to fill all the boxes with frozen turkeys, canned goods, pies, rolls, stuffing mixes, and a Thanksgiving prayer. Max helped transport the boxes to several trunks, including his own. Since he had to work the next few days, he and Gramps planned to deliver the boxes on his list this afternoon.

When he returned to the almost-empty dining room, Oliver was drawing a picture with another boy, and Gramps, Colette, and Ava were still chatting. Ava and Colette had practically become best friends since their meeting only a couple of days ago, and Ava seemed to be enjoying being with the seniors as much as they were.

As Max approached them, the color drained from Ava's face. She was looking past his shoulder and looked like she had just seen a ghost. He glanced back, but the only person behind him was Jack Sullivan.

Jack walked over to Colette and kissed her on the cheek. "It looks like you did a great job as always, Mom. Sorry I couldn't be more help with packaging this year, but my trunk is full for my deliveries."

Ava's jaw was slack as her eyes darted between Jack and Colette. Turning quickly, she almost ran as she made her way through the tables and into the bathroom. What was that all about?

Max kept watch for Ava out of his peripheral vision while he discussed Thanksgiving plans with Jack, Colette, and Gramps. The two families often shared holiday meals together, so they mostly confirmed who was bringing what and what time they were expected at Colette's house.

When Ava walked out of the bathroom, he made his way to her, took her by the elbow, and led her into the sitting room. He couldn't help but notice her tremor against his hand. The color had returned to her face, but she still looked shaken.

"Are you okay?"

The smile she put on was as fake as the wreath on the wall behind her. "Fine. Just tired. I'm fine." She was a horrible liar—a quality he appreciated in a person, especially a woman he found attractive. She glanced toward the dining room, then the door on the opposite wall that led outside. "Would you watch Oliver for a minute? I just need some air."

Without waiting for his reply, she turned and rushed toward the door. He strode into the dining room and helped Oliver get his things together, then told him to wait with Gramps.

When he walked through the door, Ava stood facing away from him. She jumped when he put his hand on her back.

"Where's Oliver?"

"He's fine. He's waiting with Gramps. Let's go get the car warmed up."

"Sure." She kept her head low and eyes on the sidewalk in front of her as they walked. He had to walk quickly to keep up with her pace, certain that if it wouldn't have caused a scene, she would have run to his car and hidden in the back seat.

When she reached the car, she got in quickly. He took his time walking to his door, giving himself a moment to process what had just happened. When he got in the car, she was sitting quietly, staring at the side mirror. He started the car but didn't move to put it in gear. "Ava, is there something I should know?"

She looked in his direction without making eye contact. "I don't know what you mean. I think the busyness of the week just caught up to me."

It was driving him crazy to see that something was going on and be powerless to do anything about it. This was starting to remind him of the memory he tried so hard to forget, the one that made him uproot his life and start over in Summit County. He wasn't going to make the mistake of not looking into things again but needed to tread carefully. "If you need something, just ask."

"I'm fine. All I need is a nap." She smiled her plastic smile again, then looked over her shoulder at the church. In his rearview mirror he saw Jack and Colette get into Jack's car and move in the opposite direction. Ava's entire posture relaxed as she exhaled.

He caught her eye, hoping she wouldn't look away again. "If something changes, tell me."

Was Jack Sullivan involved in whatever she was hiding? They weren't close, but with Max's grandmother and Colette being best friends since childhood, Max had known Jack all his life. The families were more like relatives than friends.

Jack was a beloved and respected member of the community, and Max had never had reason to question his character. So why did Ava look so nervous when he walked into the church? The one thing that he knew was that she wasn't going to tell him straight out.

The ride back to Lakes End was similar to the one to the church, with Gramps telling Oliver about the baseball leagues he used to play in. He was so happy to be sharing and reliving old memories that he didn't act like he noticed that Ava's eyes looked a million miles away, even when she nodded along with their conversation.

When Max pulled into the driveway at home, Ava seemed to come out of her daze. She looked at him quizzically as Gramps opened his door. "Ava, Oliver, it was wonderful worshipping and serving with you today. Maxwell, I'll see you when I get up."

"Bye, Mr. Vernon." Oliver was half-asleep but gave him a high-five as he got out of the car.

"See you soon, Gramps." He pulled back out of the driveway. "He's taken a twenty-minute nap every afternoon for as long as I can remember, so it was easier to drop him off first. By the time I get back from dropping you off and take the dog for a walk, he'll be ready to deliver Thanksgiving boxes."

"Okay." She was quiet on the short drive to the hotel. He had hoped that maybe if he didn't pressure her with more questions, she would open up. Instead, she withdrew further.

When he pulled up to the hotel entrance, she quickly let Oliver out and took his booster seat. Oliver looked like he was sleepwalking as he carried his seat toward the building. Max stood in front of Ava, blocking her path. "Are you in some sort of trouble?"

She gasped. "No! Of course not." She regained her composure and, along with it, her plastic smile. "Thank you for including us today. I loved your little church and helping make Thanksgiving better for families who need a hand."

"I like helping anyone who needs it." He reached out and touched her arm. "Will you tell me if you need help?"

"Thanks for a great day, Max. Take care." She bolted into the hotel lobby without looking back.

Chapter 13

AVA COULD BARELY BREATHE by the time she got back to her room. Her heart was racing so fast that she felt like she was going to pass out. Was this what a panic attack felt like?

She helped Oliver with his coat and boots. "Why don't you lie on your bed and read for a few minutes, sweetie? We've had a big day."

"Okay." Oliver had resisted naps since he was three, but when she suggested he lie down and read, he usually acquiesced. His eyes never stayed open for more than a few minutes.

She busied herself with tidying the hats, scarves, and mittens while she waited for sleep to take Oliver. It didn't take long, and she breathed a prayer of thanks to God for holding her together.

Sitting on the bed, she braced her hands on her knees. When she closed her eyes, all she could see was Jack Sullivan's face.

Her father's face.

His raven hair and green eyes were reflections of her own. Had Colette noticed the resemblance? Had Max?

Colette. The woman she had felt such an immediate connection to was her grandmother.

Her head started pounding. It was all too much to deal with. She undressed and stepped into a hot shower, wishing she could go back in time and say no to the invitation to the church. Why had she come to Michigan, anyway? What had she hoped to gain?

Why had she thought she could come to his town, spy on him from across a street for a few moments to see what he looked like, and leave without him ever seeing her?

The shower did nothing to slow her heart rate or stop her shaking hands. She let the hot water run over her face as the tears she had been holding in for two months finally burst out of her. Gasping for breath, she sat in the tub and let her tears flow.

She cried for her mother. She cried for her home and business that were taken less than a month after her mother's death by the hurricane that took so many lives but spared hers. She cried for the crazy idea she'd had to drive all the way to Michigan to get a glimpse of the man who had given her life but who had no idea she existed. She cried for Oliver, who had lost his own father when he was six months old and would never know his grandfather or great-grandmother.

By the time the tears finally dried up, she was exhausted. Despite the fact that it was not even dinner time, she wanted to go to bed. She wished she could sleep for a week. God knew she hadn't slept well since her mother's death, and she desperately needed it.

She dried her hair, staring into the mirror at the dark color. It was always a contrast to her mother's blonde and she assumed it was from her father, but seeing it was jarring. Even her green eye color was exactly like his. She had known from the picture that she resembled him, but the picture didn't prepare her for seeing that resemblance up close and personal.

Hoping Oliver would sleep for a while longer, she stretched out on her bed. Sleep took her quickly, but it did not give her the rest she was looking for. Dreams and memories played in her mind, retelling many of the most significant moments of her life.

She dreamt about the day her mother told her the truth about her conception. After believing for eighteen years that her father had been the love of her mother's life who died in a house fire before she was born, she was stunned to find out that she was conceived in a cold, sterile doctor's office. Ava had never heard of a sperm donor or known such a thing existed until the day her mother told her the truth.

Images of her mother's face contrasted with Jack's. Her mother was forty years old when she walked into that sperm bank. Jack was eighteen when he did the same.

In her dream she ran from the faces. They kept appearing in front of her. No matter how fast or far she ran, they were there. She bolted upright in her bed, covered in sweat, breathing hard.

What have I done?

It was one thing to imagine the man attached to the small bit of non-identifying information from the sperm bank and the name from GenealogyWeb. It was quite another to see the man who had a mother and a wife and children.

Pandora's box was unlocked. Was there a way to close it again and forget about the crazy idea to learn about Jack?

She had never intended to meet him. All she wanted was a glimpse from across a street. She had been certain that if she saw what he looked like and her curiosity was satisfied, she could go back home and move on with her life. Someday when she told Oliver, she could describe the man who he also resembled.

Having seen him, her curiosity was in no way satisfied. If anything, it was hungrier. It wanted more information, more time to look. She wanted to know him and wished more than anything that Oliver could.

She was flirting with disaster, and she knew it. The idea of leaving town made her feel like a giant bear was squeezing the breath out of her again.

The idea of leaving a grandmother who had already become a friend was worse. Why had God allowed her to go into that store?

Colette. Somehow because of technology and her mother's choice of a young and healthy donor, Ava had a grandmother who may be younger than her mother.

A grandmother. Why hadn't she thought of that?

She had wished for a grandmother for as long as she could remember. Her mother had been an only child and a late in life baby, so her parents died long before Ava was born. Ava carried her maternal grandmother's name but had never spent a moment in her presence.

Colette was everything Ava had ever wished for in a grandmother. She was so kind, lively, and sweet. They had such an instant and deep connection. Even Oliver was taken with her. *No wonder.*

They had even made plans while filling baskets at the church to have tea together at the shop tomorrow. How could Ava sit and enjoy a cup of tea with the woman she had to keep such an earth-shattering secret from?

The only thing worse than that was leaving town and never seeing her again. If she cancelled, she would also deprive Oliver of the chance to know his great-grandmother, even if he didn't know who she was at the time.

"Lord, what should I do? You know I never wanted to disrupt Jack's life. I just wanted to see him. It seemed so easy."

She opened her Bible and flipped through the Psalms. In the ten years since she had invited Jesus to be in her life, anytime she wanted comfort, she went to that book. The poetry was always calming, especially the verses about God being a Father to the fatherless.

She lost track of time as she read and prayed. Despite not getting any clear answers about what to do, she felt a measure of peace after spending time in God's Word.

Oliver stirred on his bed. "I'm hungry."

Time to get back into Mommy mode. "Okay, I'll make us something." She didn't have an appetite, but if she didn't eat, her blood sugar might get off-kilter. Curiosity about Jack's health sprung up in her head. Did he have the same challenges with blood sugar? Were there other health problems she should know about?

When she looked at her phone, she saw that she had missed several calls and texts in the hours since she had silenced the notifications, mostly from Sarita and Max. Both expressed concern in their voicemails. When had Max become enough of a friend that his voice gave her as much comfort as Sarita's?

Sarita threatened to call a search party if Ava didn't call back, so she answered her first. Not ready to talk about what had happened, she texted and said she and Oliver were tired after a busy day and that she was going to take Oliver to the pool and curl up with a book. The text to Max was short and sweet, despite taking twenty minutes of writing and rewriting. She finally settled on repeating what she said to Sarita and thanking him again for including them.

Chapter 14

MAX RUBBED HIS EYES. They were dry after four hours of trying to find any information he could about both Ava and Jack and coming up empty-handed. It would be a lot easier if he could run a search using the resources at work without getting fired.

Ava's profile picture on Friendline, the only social media site he found her on, was of her and a woman who must be her grandmother. They didn't resemble each other, with the woman's blonde hair a sharp contrast to Ava's, but their body language made it look like they were close. There were no pictures of Oliver, but he knew plenty of people who kept pictures of their children off the internet.

Most of the posts were about events at her store or in the historic district it was located in. There were several comments from people expressing their concern for her and sorrow about the store being destroyed, so that part of her story checked out. He could see why she supported her landlord's fight to preserve the Spanish revival building. It was beautiful, and the shops in it looked to be thriving before the hurricane tore through it on its way up the coast.

He searched through the last two years of posts and found very little that was personal. She had posted an obituary a couple of months ago, which informed him that the woman in the picture was her mother, not her grandmother. The woman was eighty-one when she died after a short illness, and there were several comments expressing condolences to Ava and Oliver.

There was not one thing that looked suspicious or out of the ordinary, and everything fit with what little she had told him. "What is your secret, Ava? What are you hiding?" He was at a loss as he tried to figure out what was going on. He had a gut feeling about her, that she was as genuine and innocent as she presented herself to be, but she was hiding something. What was it?

He took out his notepad. "Okay, let's start at the beginning. Why would someone who is innocent and truthful act so frightened and skittish? It doesn't make sense. She said she came to town for research, but what kind of research would be so secret? Could she have had some kind of relationship with Jack?" He tried to ignore the way his chest burned at the thought of her with another man. Oliver's existence was proof that she had been involved with a man at some point, and her bare ring finger and lack of mention of him gave reason to believe that he was not currently in her life. Even Oliver had said straight out that he didn't have a dad. What kind of man would give up the chance for a life with Ava and Oliver?

The way Ava acted when she saw Jack said she knew him. There was no one else in that part of the room, and she was definitely looking straight at Jack before she turned and bolted. Max had been so focused on her that he didn't notice if Jack had seen her or not.

He sat back and raked his hands through his hair. "Okay, Ava, you are as big a mystery now as you were before I started looking for information on you." Thoughts of Cecilia and the tragedy he had barely prevented goaded him. He would never allow himself to miss clues that were right under his nose again.

This was different, though. He knew that down to the very center of his gut. Ava was not Cecilia, and this wasn't the same type of situation he let himself get involved with in Flint. Ava needed help, and he was the man for the job. But what did she need help with?

Clicking over to the other tab on the screen, he continued his investigation. "Let's see about you, Jack. Are you hiding something?"

Jack had a Friendline account and he and Max were friends, but a search of his page came up with nothing. The only times any personal activity showed was when someone else tagged him in a group photo. His own social media posting was all work-related, mostly about new listings or open houses.

In the five years Max had lived in Summit County, he had seen Jack regularly at social gatherings, including the holidays their families shared, and community events. They had usually talked about hunting, fishing, and the sports Jack's younger son was coaching. Before what he saw in the church earlier, if someone would have asked Max everything he knew about Jack, he would have said he was a good man, a good husband and father, and a value to the community. Now he wondered if there was something else.

What connection could two decent, right-living people who lived in separate states possibly have?

Chapter 15

AVA SAT ON HER bed and stared at the ceiling in the hotel room the next morning, trying to decide what to do. Oliver was doing his homework and she was trying to make up for lost sleep with caffeine. Her night of sleep could be described as fitful at best, thanks to the images swirling in her head and making her feel like a jerk.

This whole plan had been foolish from the start. Where had she ever gotten the idea that seeing Jack from afar would give her any kind of closure—or even answers? It had done nothing but open up a deep cavern of emptiness inside her and made her feel worse about Oliver's lack of family.

Heaviness descended on her. Her own curiosity and selfishness had brought her on this fool's errand, and she had brought Oliver along for the ride. He had no memories of the father who died before his first birthday, but she had thought she was filling in the gap. Seeing him with Max and Vernon showed her otherwise.

Where she got the idea that she could fill in for Elliott was beyond her. The car accident that had left her a young widow had left her son in the exact same situation she had grown up in, and no amount of mothering made up for his lack of father, siblings, grandparents, and cousins.

She loved her mother dearly, but she had always felt like she was missing something by not having an extended family. It was as if she had a family-shaped hole inside of her heart. When her mother, the only family she knew, succumbed to pancreatic cancer, that hole only expanded. Since that day, Ava and Oliver existed in a world of two. They had friends, but they were still alone.

Jack had the family she had always longed for and hoped she could provide for her son. Was that what she was in Michigan for? Family? Jack's family?

The man owed her nothing, and she owed him the courtesy of not pulling the rug out from under the good life he seemed to have. She wouldn't do that to him or to his wife or children. Most of all, she wouldn't do that to Colette. Her appearance could only make waves in the family, and that was the last thing she wanted to do.

"Done." Oliver held up his completed worksheet. "Can I take my bath now?"

"Sure." She filled the tub and put his discarded clothes in the laundry bag while he picked out which toys would go on an underwater adventure.

She got dressed while he took his bath. In three hours, they were supposed to meet Colette at her store. Part of her hoped that Woody would say her car wasn't fixed so that she would have an excuse to skip the teatime visit. Thinking of missing that visit with her new friend—her new *grandmother*—made her eyes burn. She knew the best thing would be to get out of town before anyone knew the reason for her visit and before Oliver could become more attached to people he would have to leave behind. Her head knew that, at least. Her heart wanted to stay for at least a few days, spend some time with Colette, and learn about the family that belonged to her and Oliver in biology only.

And then there was Max. Why couldn't she have met him somewhere else? She desperately wanted more time with him too, both for herself and for her son.

When her phone buzzed and she saw Sarita's name on the screen, she almost cried in relief. Sarita would help her figure things out.

"Morning."

"Are you okay? If you hadn't answered, I was ready to get in the car and drive up there myself."

"Trust me, snow is no joke. You do not want to drive on these roads. I'm sorry I didn't call yesterday. I just couldn't bring myself to do it."

Her friend's voice was laced with concern. "Did something happen?"

She squeezed her eyes shut. "I saw Jack."

Sarita gasped. "You saw him? Did he see you?"

"I'm not sure. I basically turned and ran." She fought emotion as she relayed the events at the church. "Collette is his mother."

"Colette, the woman who owns the store you loved so much?"

"One and the same." If only she'd had more time with Colette before finding out.

"Wow. Just wow, Ava. Do you want me to come up there?"

Despite the fact that they weren't on a video call, Ava shook her head. "No. I'm coming home as soon as I have my car."

Sarita spoke in the *I-mean-business* tone she used on her kids. "No."

"What do you mean, no?"

She took a long breath. "You're going to regret it if you leave without getting what you went there for. I can hear it in your voice."

Ava slumped onto the bed. "But I don't really know what I came here for."

"I think you do. You were looking for information at the bare minimum. Now that you know where to get it, get what you can. You could find out all about your family without them being the wiser."

"I just don't want to hurt anybody in the process." *Or get hurt myself when I have to leave.*

"Then be careful. Don't interrogate his mother, but ask her some questions and get her to talk about the family."

Ava sighed. "It really would be wonderful to spend some more time with her before I go."

"And Max?"

She twisted her ring as she pictured his warm brown eyes . . . that dimple . . . the arms she longed to be wrapped in . . .

"Ava?"

"Sorry. I got lost in a moment."

"It sounds like you need more time with him too."

She smiled. "I probably shouldn't because it will make it harder to leave, but I want it. He's really wonderful to both of us. And his grandpa . . ."

Sarita's voice was firm. "Then stay."

The phone beeped with an incoming call from Woody. "Hang on a minute, Sarita. This is about the car."

Woody's news that the car was ready was welcome, as was the price. She very much liked small-town prices. When Woody said that Max had offered to pick her up on his lunch break and was probably on his way, she felt her pulse jump. Not having a good excuse to say no—or wanting to say no—she thanked Woody and said goodbye.

Sarita sounded nervous when Ava clicked back to their call. "Is it ready?"

"Yes, and it's not going to break the bank. I should bring my car here for all of its servicing needs."

"That's great. Now back to what we were talking about. Will you stay for a few more days?"

"Yes. I'll stay for a couple more days, then head home."

"Wait. What about Thanksgiving?"

Ava's breath caught. She didn't even want to think about it. "Thanksgiving is going to be the first holiday without my mom, so it's probably good to spend it in a hotel room on the way back. Maybe if I focus on the drive and eat anything but turkey, I'll forget what day it is."

"I can pack Enrique and the kids in the van and we'll come meet you. You and Oliver should be with family."

Tears stung her eyes. She and Oliver didn't have a family anymore. Sarita's family was *like* family, but that wasn't the same. She swallowed the lump in her throat. "Thank you, but no. We'll be fine." She stood and started pacing again. Her ride would be there soon, which gave her two great reasons to end the call. "I need to go. Max is going to pick us up and drive us to my car."

"Don't change the subject. I don't want you to be alone on Thanksgiving." Sarita was truly the best friend Ava could ever ask for.

"Thank you and I love you, but this is what I need this year. I'll call you later, okay?" She ended the call before Sarita could argue.

Wiping her eyes, she focused on getting ready for her ride. As she brushed her hair and touched up her eye makeup, she thought about what Sarita had said. She was right. It wouldn't hurt to spend a couple more days getting to know about her family and spending time with Max.

If she left on Thanksgiving morning, that would give her this afternoon plus two full days to spend as much time as she could with

Colette and Max. She closed her eyes and took a deep breath. "Lord, please help me to let go of the things I can't have and to enjoy the next few days. Help Oliver and me to make some great memories and help me to learn all I can."

Chapter 16

MAX'S STOMACH DID A flip when Ava walked out of the hotel with a smile on her face. *Keep it in check, man. You don't know her well yet.*

He needed to stay focused this time. That meant he couldn't let his feelings get in the way of his investigation. Now that her car was ready, this might be his last chance to get any information. He couldn't think about how he was going to miss having the chance to chauffeur them around.

Oliver was several steps behind her, and when he saw the patrol car, he let out a whoop and ran to it in a full sprint. "We get to ride in the police car again?"

"We sure do."

Ava grinned as he took the booster seat and secured it in the car. "You're making his year, you know."

He opened the passenger door before she could get into the back seat with Oliver.

"Isn't this against protocol?" She looked so innocent that Max laughed.

The fact that she wasn't kidding made her question funnier. "It's fine."

Having the reminder that she seemed to be such a goody two-shoes kicked his curiosity into a higher gear. He prayed for divine help as he walked back to his side of the car.

"Thank you for another ride. You should send me a bill." Her smile was warm, which in turn warmed him.

"Mom, take pictures with your eyes up there so you can tell me how to draw stuff later."

"Sure thing, sweetie."

"I take it you're feeling better?"

She nodded. "Yes, and I'm relieved to get my car back without having to sell a kidney."

This time he couldn't hold back his laugh. "Woody just takes cash or credit—no organs."

"That's a relief."

He didn't want to spend the whole ride talking about her transportation. If he was going to be able to help her at all, he had a job to do.

"So, you're going to have a visit with Colette?"

She grinned. "Yes. You know her well, right?"

"All my life."

"Then do you know if she likes scones? I thought about getting some from the bakery on my way to her shop."

He reached into his memory bank, trying to come up with an answer for her. "I know she makes delicious desserts, but I have absolutely no idea about scones. You really like her, huh?"

Her eyes looked misty when she answered. "She's amazing." He had heard of couples falling in love at first site, but never friends. Maybe it was because Ava missed her mother that she became attached to Colette so quickly. It must be especially rough facing the holidays after losing her.

Focus. Get answers.

With Oliver too focused on the equipment in the police car to listen to their conversation, this was his chance, but he was at a loss. It was a good thing he never had any big dreams about being a detective, because one look into her eyes sent him flailing. The hours he had spent on the computer last night had done nothing to help him.

Wait. It was in front of him all along. *Colette.* Was Colette the key to Ava's trip? Had Ava reacted to Jack only because he was Colette's son?

He frowned. Now he was just pulling at strings. Max was the one who took Ava to Colette's store the first time, and Max was the one who invited her to Colette's church. Not getting answers was starting to make him delusional.

He needed more time with her. "Gramps asked me to convince you two to come for dinner tonight. He's making his famous chili."

"Oh, I—"

"Unless you need to work on your research." Whatever the research was, she couldn't have gotten much done with her car in the shop and him on her tail.

She looked at him and smiled. "No, it will be fine. We'd love to see those bookshelves you made."

Did she really say yes? No argument? No excuse?

He grinned at her. "How about if I pick you up after work? For old times' sake."

Her laugh made him wish it was a date. He might do just about anything to hear that sound more—anything short of giving up his own investigation.

Ava was afraid of something and, if anything, he needed to step up the investigation. If she was in trouble, he was going to be there to protect her and Oliver. This time he would come through, and not when it was almost too late.

Disappointment hit when he pulled into Woody's parking lot. She looked like she might be feeling it too. Wasn't it just yesterday when she couldn't get out of his car fast enough? The woman was a mystery.

She flashed that beautiful smile at him as she got out of the car. "Thanks for the ride, Officer Brody. See you tonight."

I'll be counting the hours. He watched her go as he opened the rear door for Oliver. "You wanna sit up front with me for a couple of minutes, champ?"

Oliver's eyes almost popped out of his head. "I can?"

"You can, as long as you don't touch anything. But if you point at something, I'll tell you what it is."

The boy scrambled into the front seat. "Cool!"

Chapter 17

IT FELT GOOD TO be back behind the wheel of her own car. Ava had to work to focus on the road in front of her, because all she could see was Max's smile as she got out of his patrol car. *If only—no. We're not going to think about that. We're going to enjoy every second of the next few days with him and store up memories of Colette for a lifetime.*

Oliver's nonstop chatter about riding in the police car, and especially his time in the front seat while Ava was talking to Woody and paying, became white noise as she made her way through the unfamiliar town. Turning down Main Street, she looked for the bakery. She was certain it was close to Colette's shop.

Finding it, they ran in to see what would still be available this late in the day. The moment they crossed the threshold, they were met by the smell of coffee, butter, and sugar. The place was almost empty, so she was free to take her time looking at the display case without holding anyone up—or having to hide her face.

To her great delight, they had both lemon and almond scones. To Oliver's, they had chocolate donuts. While the order was being boxed up, she noticed a fresh apple cake. "What do you think, Ollie? Should we take that for dessert at Officer Max and Mr. Vernon's?"

He nodded enthusiastically. "Yum."

When she approached Up North Clothing and Treasures, she walked slowly and looked inside to make sure Jack wasn't there. Seeing only a woman talking with Colette, she walked in, scones in hand.

Colette greeted her with a wide smile. "Ava! Were your ears burning? I was just talking about you." She pointed behind the cash register to where she had framed the picture Oliver had drawn for her. "And Oliver, the artist in residence!"

The woman she was talking to was younger than Ava and had a style all her own, part punk rocker and part Kate Middleton. She looked somewhat familiar when she turned and greeted Ava with a warm smile and extended hand. "Ava, Grandma has told me so much about you. I'm Kara."

Kara. Ava hoped no one noticed her sharp inhale at the woman's name. Of course she looked familiar. It was Kara.

Kara, the one who had her privacy settings open enough on GenealogyWeb that she led Ava to Jack.

Kara, Jack's daughter.

Kara, her sister.

"Hi," Ava stammered, reaching back to shake her hand. "It's nice to meet you. This is my son, Oliver." Should she run? If she stayed, she would be lying to both Colette and Kara. But how could she leave now that she already felt a connection with them?

"Are you okay?" Colette looked concerned.

She brushed off the question with a smile. "Yes, of course. I'm just adjusting to the cold and wishing I had brought another scone for your granddaughter."

Kara waved her off. "No scones for me, but thank you. I've got to work the rest of the afternoon, and those make my blood sugar go all funny."

So the blood sugar thing does run in the family. If Ava wasn't sure about the ethics of her research trip before, she was now. Beyond wanting to know them, she needed medical information for herself and for Oliver.

Ava reached into her purse and pulled out a bag of almonds. "I get that sometimes too. Can I offer you some almonds instead?"

Kara and Colette shared a look and laughed together, then Kara pulled her own stash from her purse. "I never leave home without them."

"You know what they say about great minds." Colette smiled at Kara. "I told you that you would like her."

"I never doubted it for a second."

Ava fought to act normal in the midst of being overwhelmed by what she was experiencing. She tried to be subtle while studying Kara. Kara's red hair and creamy complexion were nothing like her own. She must take after her mother. Standing and talking with her grandmother and sister was like a dream come true. Her mission wasn't just about Jack, as she had so naively thought. It was about the whole family.

The three women sat and chatted over tea, with Colette and Kara taking turns tending to customers and Oliver drawing pictures for them like he did in her shop. Ava was fascinated watching the closeness between the two women, and she felt the same instant bond with Kara as she had Colette, especially when Kara sat on the floor and drew a picture with Oliver. Ava liked her spunky nature, and it was clear she also adored Colette.

When a woman about Ava's age wandered in with a furrowed brow that Ava recognized as belonging to a stressed shopper, she signaled to Colette to stay seated while she waited on her. Ava strode over and greeted her. "You look like you're in a hurry. Can I help you save some time?"

The woman looked at her, relieved. "Yes, I hope so. I need a small gift for a mother-in-law who hates everything I buy."

Ava gave her a knowing smile. "So something safe, unique, and not too pricey?"

She chuckled. "Yes, I've learned not to waste too much money on something she's going to look down her nose at."

"I've got the perfect idea." Ava gestured to the woman to follow her to the impulse buy section. "These beeswax candles smell divine, and they look much more expensive than they are. I've watched three women buy these in the two times I've been in this store."

The woman's head snapped toward Ava. "Oh! You don't work here?"

"No, but I have a gift shop in Miami and I miss helping customers." She gestured toward Colette, who was watching and smiling. "I wanted to give my friend a break and let her enjoy her tea."

The woman sniffed the candle and sighed. "This is beautiful, and the scent won't knock her out. She'll have a hard time hating it." She set it on the counter. "You don't gift wrap by any chance, do you?"

"We do." Ava walked behind the counter and pulled the wrapping supplies from where she had seen Colette put them. She wrapped the gift as Colette walked over and rang up the order.

Colette smiled at the woman. "The gift wrapping is on the house today. Call it our cranky mother-in-law discount."

The woman laughed. "You've just made my day. I'll be back when I have time to shop for myself."

"I look forward to it."

Oliver ran over to the woman. "Would you like a picture, free of charge?" He gave his most charming smile.

"I would love one." She bent down to take it and ruffled his hair. "What a beautiful tree! Are you sure you don't want to give this to your mom?"

"No, she has plenty." He was a pro at working customers. "This one is for you."

When the woman left the store with a smile on her face, Colette turned to Ava. "Oh, how I wish you lived here. I would pay you anything you wanted to work here."

Kara stood and picked up her purse. "I need to get back to the salon, Grandma."

She hugged Colette, then Ava. "It was great meeting you, Ava. I hope you're staying in town for a while and I can see you again."

I wish I could. "It was wonderful meeting you too."

"Bye, Oliver." She bent down to give him a fist bump. "Stay cool and keep drawing!"

Ava blinked back tears as she watched Kara walk out the door. *This is going to be harder than I thought.*

When she noticed Colette looking at her, she scrambled for something to say. "Your shop is wonderful. Do you stay open all year? I noticed several stores on the street were closed for the winter."

Colette glanced toward the front of the store. "Mine is usually closed by now too. I usually spend six months here and six months in Phoenix near my other son and his family, but this year I decided to stay through Christmas. There's something wonderful about the holidays in the snow."

Ava smiled. "I would imagine so."

Colette's face fell as she gazed around the room. "My sons are begging me to sell the store. They think I'm too old to work."

"And you disagree."

Her shoulders straightened. "I most certainly do. I can't do as much as I used to, but I'm not ready to sit around and knit. My boys forget that they got their work ethic from both of their parents." She shook her head. "I could use some more help, but it will be enough to hire an assistant manager next spring."

She walked back to the sitting area and topped off their cups. "Tell me more about your store."

It was evident that Colette did not want to talk any further about closing hers. She obviously loved the place too much to let it go easily. If only Ava could keep her secret and move to Hideaway. She would gladly work for minimum wage for the chance to spend more time with her grandmother and to give Oliver the chance to really know the woman.

Reminding herself of her mission to enjoy every minute she could with the people who had come to mean so much to her, she sat back and lifted her tea. She was determined to have a nice afternoon with her grandmother. Time was short.

Chapter 18

MAX ARRIVED AT THE hotel as quickly as he could after work. He had barely made it out of the station on time, thanks to Mrs. Morrison's complaint about the deer crossing through her yard. It had required all of his patience to calmly explain that wildlife didn't follow zoning or traffic laws. By the time he sent her on her way with a gentle pat on the back, he was almost late.

Ava and Oliver were waiting inside the lobby, and when they walked out the door, she greeted him with the kind of smile that turned a man to mush. There was something about her—strong and independent, yet fragile and vulnerable—that drew him in more than any other woman in recent memory had. Even though she had her secrets and was dealing with something that frightened her, she seemed completely comfortable in who she was and exuded the kind of grace that made every woman beautiful. He needed to be on his game if he was going to stay on track and get information tonight when all he wanted to do was get her to smile at him again. Oliver was tugging at his heart too. The boy was all innocence, curiosity, and enthusiasm, and Max was enjoying his time with him as much as with Ava.

"Thank you for being our chauffeur again." She looked outside at the snow that was starting to fall. "I guess it's best that I'm not driving tonight."

"I'm not sure about that. I have it on good authority that you aced your driving lesson."

She chuckled. "All the same, I think I'm more comfortable being a passenger when it's snowing."

"Can we spin again, Officer Max?"

"Not tonight, champ. But I think my grandpa has some things he wants to show you when we get there."

"What kind of things?"

Max met his eyes in the rearview mirror and wiggled his brows. "Baseball things."

Ava mouthed the word as Oliver exclaimed, "Cool!" The boy did have an affinity for that word.

During most of the drive to his house, while Oliver talked about his favorite things about baseball, Ava looked out the window. This time it didn't seem like she was avoiding looking at him. She was gazing at the snowflakes that were starting to cover the trees.

"Is it safe to be driving tonight?"

He snickered. "We're only supposed to get a few inches tonight. Around here, we call that a dusting."

Even as she laughed, she looked like she was trying to gauge whether or not he was kidding.

"Scout's honor. It will be fine. By the way, how do you feel about dogs?"

"We love them."

Oliver added, "I want a dog, but Mom said no."

Ava looked at him sheepishly. "In my defense, we don't have a living situation conducive to having a pet. I do love them though. Why?"

"I was hoping I didn't have to kennel mine during your visit."

"Oh, you definitely don't. What kind is it?"

"He's a German Shepherd."

Oliver filled in the rest from his spot in the back seat. "His name is Zeus and he was a police officer like Officer Max."

She turned in her seat to face her son. "How do you know so much about him?"

"When you were taking too long to pay the man and get the car, Officer Max showed me his picture. He helps find lost people in the woods."

"That's an important job." She turned her gaze to Max. "Is he friendly?"

He grinned. "As long as you're not coming at me or my grandpa with intent to harm, he'll be your best friend."

Zeus's head popped up in the front window when Max pulled into the driveway. He stood at attention, watching Max's every move as they got out of the car.

Ava eyed him warily. "He looks scary."

"He's trained to. He was my partner in Flint." Max held out his hand for Oliver and arm for Ava to hold while they walked on the uneven concrete slabs that led to the front door.

"He's really a police dog?" She looked back at Zeus.

"I told you, Mom."

"Yes, you did."

Max leaned close. "He's retired, but don't tell him."

"His secret is safe with me." She pulled her fingers across her lips like a zipper.

Ava slowed down her stride and examined the front porch. "I love your farmhouse! So fashionable."

He gave her a sideways glance. "Please, I beg you—don't call it cute."

She covered her mouth when she laughed. "I just meant that the farmhouse style is fashionable these days. I didn't mean to offend or insinuate that you were following decorating trends."

He met her smile as he opened the front door and gestured to Zeus to stay. "We've got two men and a dog living here, so I assure you, it's not fashionable. Definitely not cute."

As they stepped over the threshold, they were met by the smell of chili and cornbread. "It smells great in here, Gramps."

"Vernon, it smells wonderful."

Gramps called from the kitchen. "I'll be out in a minute when the cornbread is done. Sorry, I wasn't able to do much with Zeus before you got here."

Max walked over to him and scratched him behind the ears. "You need some drills, bud?"

Ava held Oliver where she was. "Will he be okay with us petting him?"

"Sure. He's been out of regular duty long enough that he's more comfortable around people. Zeus, this is Ava and Oliver. They're new friends." Zeus slowly approached them and sniffed their outstretched hands, then soaked up all the attention they lavished on him without taking his eyes off Max.

"I need to take him outside for a couple of drills. Would you like to join us or stay inside?"

"I wanna go outside with Zeus!" The boy could hardly stand still.

Ava's eyes widened. "Drills? Is he in training?"

"Police dogs are always in training. They get depressed when they don't have jobs, so he runs drills a couple of times a day and goes to work with me now and then." He opened the front door. "He's still great at search and rescue when hikers and hunters get stranded in the woods."

"Wow. I'd like to watch, if it's okay with Zeus."

The way the dog was standing between her and Oliver, his answer was clear.

"Looks like he wants to impress you. Come on, Zeus, let's go to work." As Zeus ran out the door with Oliver following, Max turned to Ava. "Would you like to help?"

She smiled. "I would love to. Tell me what to do."

He reached into the case in the front closet and held out a bullet. "Hide this somewhere on your person."

"A bullet—" Her eyes widened as she looked out at the waiting dog. "I don't want him to think I'm a criminal. I want him to like me."

Max almost doubled over in laughter. "He already likes you, and his work is a game to him. The only people he would identify as criminals are ones who come after me. You're still on his good list."

"Well in that case . . ." She took the bullet and, after appearing to consider a few hiding places, stuck it into the side of her boot. "What now?"

"Just walk outside and act natural." As soon as they got close to where Zeus was standing, he alerted Max to the bullet.

"Show me."

Zeus dutifully stared at Ava's boot.

"Good job, deputy." Max scratched Zeus and gave him a treat. Zeus sat on alert and watched as Max patted Ava's calf. Max tried not to think about the fact that he was groping her leg, and he hoped she wasn't uncomfortable with him touching her. He probably should have warned her about that part of the game.

When he pulled the bullet out, he gave Zeus more praise.

Oliver's eyes couldn't have gotten wider as he watched Zeus perform. "Cool! Can I hide something?"

"Sure. First, let's distract him. Can you throw that stick?"

Oliver threw the stick about ten feet away and Zeus ran for it.

"Nice throw, champ. Now take this and hide it in your pocket."

Oliver did as he was told and when Zeus returned, he alerted Max. Oliver giggled but stood as still as a statue while Max patted him down. Max repeated the process of praise and Oliver mimicked the way he petted him.

Ava stood still, watching. "He's fast at finding contraband and looks young. Why is he r-e-t-i-r-e-d?"

Max threw the ball he had also brought outside, and Zeus sprinted after it with Oliver on his tail. "He injured his leg in the line of duty." He shook away the memory of the night the bullet grazed Zeus's leg before it settled in Max's side.

"Really?" She looked with concern at the dog. "He doesn't act injured."

"He's perfectly healthy now. It was protocol to retire a dog if anything limited its mobility. Even though he only nicked a ligament, it ended his career." That day almost ended Max's career too—and his life. All because Max had missed clues that were right in front of him.

"And you got to keep him?"

Max smiled. "Also protocol. Their handler gets to keep them if they want to. He and I moved up here and as far as he knows, we're both small town cops. He mostly patrols the yard for mice and other critters here, and at work he helps find lost hikers and patrols cubicles for treats."

"Nice work if you can get it. How did he get injured?"

Max wasn't ready to tell that story just yet. Plus, he needed to get Ava's story. "I'll tell you my story when you tell me yours."

She inhaled sharply. Max stepped forward and put his hand on her arm. "I'd like to help if I can."

They shared a long look before Gramps rang the dinner bell. Zeus sprinted past them, not wasting a minute when his bowl waited for him, and Oliver followed.

Max smiled at her. "Saved by the bell, huh?"

She shivered. "Something like that."

"Sorry, I didn't mean to pressure you."

"It's okay. I didn't mean to pry."

When they walked into the kitchen, Gramps was putting the cornbread on the table. Max picked up the heavy pot of chili and carried it over while Gramps hugged Ava.

"Thank you for having us, Vernon. It smells amazing in here."

"Thank you, my dear." Gramps prayed over the meal, then served Ava first. "So, Ava, tell us more about yourself."

Chapter 19

AVA ALMOST CHOKED ON her chili. She had been so distracted by being in a warm and inviting home and playing with Zeus that she forgot about all of her strategies for evading questions.

She answered honestly, hoping to pivot the conversation before either of the men asked too many follow-up questions. "There's not much to tell. I grew up outside of Miami and, after the building that housed both our home and shop was damaged by Hurricane Yolanda, Oliver and I took this vacation to my mom's home state."

Oliver looked up from his bowl of chili only long enough to say, "We're on an adventure."

Vernon continued his polite query. "Your mother didn't want to come with you?"

Ava looked down and adjusted her napkin as she blinked away the heat from behind her eyes. "She died shortly before the hurricane. I'm thankful that she didn't have to see the destruction." She looked back at Vernon. "How about you? Have you lived here long?"

"Born and raised right here in this house."

She looked around the kitchen, studying the solid cabinets and counters. "Wow. Such history."

Max sat smiling at her. "Gramps remodeled the whole kitchen as a surprise before he and Grandma inherited the house."

"Very impressive." She tapped him on the arm. "And romantic."

"My dear wife said the only way she would move into my mother's house was if it could feel like hers." Vernon's slight blush was endearing.

Max grinned. "She always said this was her favorite room because she could love her family through food."

"This chili definitely tastes like it was made with love, right, Oliver?"

Unable to talk with a mouth full of cornbread, he simply nodded.

It was a delight to see how Vernon's eyes shone when his late wife was the topic of conversation. He clearly still missed her and seemed to love to tell stories. He also loved to tell stories about Max, much to Max's chagrin. She saw humility to the point of embarrassment when Vernon talked about Max's many talents and about what a help he had been in the five years since he had moved to Lakes End.

After dinner, Vernon and Max showed off each other's handiwork in the house. Oliver was fascinated at the concept of making furniture and cupboards. He rubbed his hand along the desk that Vernon's father made. "Yolanda broke my desk."

Ava explained, "Oliver had his own desk in my shop, and he drew pictures for customers there. Not much survived, and unfortunately his desk was crushed under other debris."

"We already got new crayons and markers and pencils and paper, and we're gonna find a new desk when we get home." He furrowed his brow. "I need to get back to work soon. My customers probably miss me."

The adults all tried to stifle their laughter at Oliver's seriousness about his duties. She put her hand on his shoulder. "I'm sure his customers miss him and his pictures. Oliver is my right-hand man at the shop, so he does need a place to work."

Night came too soon and before they knew it, they were headed back to the hotel. Ava didn't want the evening to end. It had been such a relief to enjoy her time with Max, and seeing him with Oliver, his grandfather, and his dog made her wish circumstances were different. He was a kind, compassionate, and loyal man. The type she could envision herself spending her life with, and the type she could envision showing Oliver how to be a good man.

When he walked them to the hotel door, he held her close, allegedly to make sure she didn't slip on the snowy ground. With his arm wrapped around her, she felt safe and secure for the first time in —she didn't know how long. Maybe the first time ever. She didn't have to perform or be perfect or be careful. She could just be. There was a sense of freedom being with him.

When they got to the door, he turned her to face him without taking his arm from her waist. His brown eyes were warm as he looked into hers. "Can I see you tomorrow?"

Oliver tugged on her hand. "Can we, Mom? I want to teach Zeus a trick."

She wished she could see Max for a string of tomorrows. Spending the evening in his home talking and laughing and hearing old stories was everything she imagined having a family would be. It was more than that, though. The way he looked at her and held her made her feel light and warm and . . . happy. When had she last felt that? Had she? Her marriage had been good, but Elliott had never set her heart or her senses on fire the way Max did.

She couldn't forget that even though she had given herself a few days to spend with Max and Colette, she and Oliver were still leaving. Her hand felt at home as it rested on his chest. "I would love that, I really would . . ."

"But . . ."

"But I can't get involved." She dropped her gaze. "We're leaving on Thursday."

His brows furrowed. "Thursday is Thanksgiving. Why don't you stay and spend it with us?"

She shook her head. "That's a family day."

"All the more reason to stay. Grandpa and I will be with Colette and her family. There's always room for two more at Colette's table."

Colette and her family. Tears stung her eyes again and she tried to blink them away. "It's for the best." She was already risking everything by staying as long as she had. If only she could hide in Max's town. If only Max's town wasn't next to Jack's. If only . . .

He ran his finger along her hair, brushing back the strands the wind had tossed. "Then let's enjoy the time we have between now and then."

You shouldn't do this. Despite the protest of her internal voice and every bit of common sense she possessed, she found herself nodding. "I would like that."

He held her tightly and lightly brushed her temple with his lips. "It's a date then. Zeus is working tomorrow, so we'll pick you up."

She lingered in his arms for a moment, savoring his strength. "I'm looking forward to it."

He nudged Oliver's shoulder. "Be ready to practice that trick with Zeus and learn how to make a snowman, Ollie."

"I will." Oliver pulled at her arm. "Come on, Mom. Let's go inside and go to bed so tomorrow gets here. G'night, Officer Max!"

Chapter 20

MAX GRIPPED THE STEERING wheel. What was he doing? He was on shaky ground at best.

It was foolish to open his heart to someone who was keeping secrets, not to mention someone who was leaving town soon. He hardly knew her, but he desperately wanted her to stay. It wasn't even just Ava, which complicated everything. He wanted Oliver to stay too. The boy was everything Max had always wanted in a son.

Having them at his place made him feel at home there for the first time. There had been an emptiness there since his grandmother passed six years ago, but with them there the house felt full. He could so easily picture spending more evenings like that with them.

When he'd finally given up his futile attempts to get information from her at dinner, they had both relaxed. Ava had such an infectious laugh and smile, and some of the stories she and Oliver told about the tourists and regulars at her store had all of them laughing. It was clear that she loved her work and that she was a gift to the neighborhood that held her store. He could only imagine the light that Oliver brought to people when he offered his pictures to them. Watching Gramps with Oliver reminded Max of his growing-up years. Gramps had poured into him more than his own father had time to, and the things he had learned at the man's feet made him who he was.

If Ava was intent on leaving on Thursday morning, he was going to make sure he spent as much time as he could with them on Tuesday and Wednesday. He didn't bother telling himself that it was just about the investigation anymore. He still wanted to know what Ava's secret was and what she was afraid of, still wanted to protect her. But more than that, he just wanted a chance to get to know her.

Gramps was reading the paper in his recliner by the fire when Max returned. The room seemed empty again. Zeus followed Max until he sat in his favorite chair, then sat at his feet.

Gramps looked up from his paper. "She's a nice girl, Maxwell. Be careful."

Did Gramps sense something that Max was missing? Was he blinded by a woman again?

"Careful?"

Gramps put the paper down and took off his glasses. "She's leaving. Best to keep that in mind before you fall too hard for her."

"What makes you think I'm falling for her?"

The old man chuckled. "For starters, I only need these glasses for reading."

"I'm not falling for anything. I'm just enjoying the company of an interesting woman."

"Don't forget pretty." He lifted up his glasses. "Only for reading."

When Gramps went to bed, Max stretched out his legs on the ottoman and watched the fire. *I'm not falling, am I?*

There was no question that he enjoyed spending time with her, but he also had a job to do. She was clearly not a threat to his town, but she was hiding her secrets well. Other than her reaction to Jack, she hadn't given him a clue to go on. Or had she?

He thought over the few things she had shared over the course of the evening. There was no mention of her father, but her mother was an estate attorney and Ava and Oliver clearly adored her. He was relieved when Ava told them about her mother's death. The closer they got, the more uncomfortable he became with knowing information about her that she hadn't shared with him.

During her visit to the house, she talked about everything that he had discovered in his evening of internet searching. She was an open book about her life, with the glaring exception of the reason for her trip to Summit County.

Zeus had taken to her immediately, and that counted for something. The dog had, after all, warned Max about Cecilia in his own way. He hadn't alerted the way he would if he smelled anything he was trained to find, but he had acted edgy around her, even going so far as to try to herd Max when she was near. With Ava and Oliver, Zeus had acted as relaxed as he did when he was just with Max and Gramps.

He pulled out his phone to try to search again. Maybe if he searched and learned more about her mother, there would be some kind of trail he could follow.

All that Ava said about her was true from what he could see. The only thing Ava had held back on was some of the accolades her mother had gotten and the impact she had on her community and church. It wasn't just Ava or Oliver who was affected by her loss.

Just as he was acknowledging the futility of his search, Zeus walked over, took the phone out of his hand, turned in a circle, then gave it back to him. Max stood up. "Okay, let's go do a perimeter check. We'll see if we can find any critters to chase."

The dog's tail wagged as he trotted to the door. One of the advantages of living in an old house where the nearest neighbor was a quarter mile away was the entertainment for Zeus. Working dogs got bored easily, and Max would much rather have Zeus hunt mice than his phone.

He did his own internal reconnaissance while walking the dog through the trees on the property, recounting the facts he had gathered so far. It didn't take long for him to recount the way she fit into his arms or the feel of her soft skin against his lips.

Chapter 21

ON TUESDAY MORNING WHILE Oliver worked on his schoolwork then drew a stack of pictures of Zeus, Ava wrote down everything she could remember from her time with Colette and Kara. She had almost filled the small notebook she brought along by the time she finished. While she was writing, she prayed, asking God to help her to remember the smallest details. Those details were going to have to last her a lifetime and they would be the only thing she could give to Oliver about his family, so she didn't want to forget a thing.

While she was writing, it was a constant battle to focus on those details instead of the ones from last night with Max. She had never met anyone she felt so comfortable with so quickly—or so attracted to so quickly. And the way he was with Oliver . . . *Why couldn't I have met someone like him in Florida, Lord? Why does he have to live near Jack?*

Sarita was right. It wouldn't hurt to enjoy her time with Max or to let Oliver spend some time around a good man. She and Oliver had every right to make some great memories here. She showered and dressed, more determined than ever to squeeze every last drop of goodness out of her time in Michigan. On the way to Colette's store, they stopped at the bakery again. This time Oliver got a donut loaded with sprinkles and she bought a variety of teatime treats.

As they were on their way out, they saw Max and Zeus walking down the sidewalk. "Zeus! Officer Max!" Oliver pulled on her jacket. "Look, Mommy."

Max flashed her a smile that made her knees—and her resolve to not get too involved—go weak. Zeus looked to Max for direction.

"Go ahead, say hi."

Zeus trotted over to where they were standing and, after receiving hugs and scratches from Oliver, sniffed around her boot. "That's a good memory you've got there, Zeus." She petted him with her free hand. "No contraband today—and I promise I'm not a criminal."

She smiled up at Max. "Good afternoon, Officer Brody."

He laughed. "You know I warned you about calling me that."

She shrugged and winked. Since when did she flirt? He took her hand and softly kissed it. "Would you two like to join us for our walk? I'm taking him to the park for a few minutes of article searching."

The day was warmer than any they'd had in Michigan, and the sun was shining overhead. Oliver looked at her with his most effective pleading expression. "Can we?"

"We'd love to. Isn't the park just past Colette's shop?"

"Indeed it is."

"Show the way then."

When they got to the park, Ava and Oliver distracted Zeus with sticks while Max threw some training toys toward all four corners of the space. Oliver followed Zeus every step of the way as he collected the toys. It was cold enough that the small park was empty, but with the sun shining and Max at her side, she was plenty warm.

She was glad she'd been unable to decide in the bakery and bought enough goodies to share. "May I offer you a donut, or would that be too stereotypical?"

"Stereotypical or not, I don't say no to anything from there." He wiggled his eyebrows toward the box. "What kind of offerings do you have?"

"You can have your pick of anything except the keto muffin."

"Is that your favorite?"

"No, that's for Kara if I see her."

He smiled, but looked like he was studying her.

She explained, "She said she has a blood sugar thing."

"Ah, I see. I'll take this then." He picked up the peanut-covered one that Ava had planned on eating herself. "My favorite."

She made a mental note to go back and get another one before she left town so that she could try one too.

He must have read her disappointment. "Have you tried these?"

She shook her head. "Not yet."

"Not trying the nutty donut from there is criminal." He broke it in half and handed her a piece. "Take it."

When she took a bite and the cakey bit of Heaven melted in her mouth, she nodded in his direction and gave a thumbs up. "I see why it's your favorite. That's delicious."

Zeus deposited each of the training toys at Max's feet. When he had retrieved all of them twice and been duly praised, Max turned to her with a sheepish smile. "We need to get back to the station. Be hungry and dress warmly when I pick you up in a few hours."

She saluted him then took Oliver's hand and started toward Colette's shop. "Aye-aye. Is your grandpa cooking again?"

"I thought we might go someplace where Zeus and Oliver can run around a bit. I'll bring dinner with me, and the dress code is casual."

"Warm and casual. Sounds intriguing. See you then." Sarita would be so proud if she saw her making plans. And looking forward to them.

ele

A few hours later, Ava got their coats while Oliver put away his art supplies. Ava hated leaving Colette's shop, but couldn't very well stay all day without raising questions.

Colette's phone rang. "Don't leave yet. My daughter-in-law is probably calling to talk about our baking plans for tomorrow afternoon. It will just be a second."

"We'll wait."

"Hi, Amanda . . . Are you ready for—oh, dear. Is he alright?"

Ava's breath caught. Had something happened to Jack?

Colette frowned. "Of course, honey. You'll be a big help to him . . . No, don't worry about a thing. You drive safe and take good care of your dad. I'll see you when you get back."

Ava exhaled. *Not Jack.* More relieved than she had a right to be, she walked over to the counter where Colette stood. "Is everything okay?"

"It's nothing serious, but Amanda's father fell off a ladder putting up Christmas decorations a couple of hours ago. She and Jack are going to go check on him and see what they can do to help for a few days."

"I'm so sorry to hear that."

Colette chuckled. "Not as sorry as he'll be when Amanda finishes with him. She told him to leave the lights for Jack to do next weekend."

"Is there anything I can do to help?"

The gleam returned to Colette's eye. "You can take Amanda's place in my kitchen tomorrow afternoon and come for Thanksgiving. The table will feel empty without Jack and Amanda there, and you two are just the ones to fill it."

She pictured the scene, sitting around her grandmother's table with her brothers and sister. She could almost smell the turkey and stuffing. How could she say no to that?

Chapter 22

TIME PASSED SLOWLY AFTER the surprise visit with Ava and Oliver during the afternoon. The town was quiet and people seemed to be behaving themselves, so Max spent most of his time catching up with paperwork and keeping Zeus from pestering his coworkers.

He called the Rock Creek Tavern and ordered three of their least messy sandwiches before leaving work, then picked them up on the way to the hotel. He had also showered and changed clothes, despite having Zeus there. If he could don civilian attire before leaving the station to fool a dog, he could do it to impress a lady.

When he saw Ava and Oliver standing at the door of the hotel, he wanted nothing more than to cover the boy's eyes and plant a kiss on her that would make her hair curl. She was not a woman to be toyed with or pushed into anything, though, and he was determined not to fall, so he summoned all of his restraint and stuck to a polite hand on her back as he ushered them to the car. He was getting more adept at securing Oliver's booster seat, and the boy squealed in excitement when he saw that he was sharing the back seat with Zeus.

Ava took a deep breath. "It smells like dinner in here. Are we having a picnic?"

"If that's okay with you. I thought you might enjoy one of my favorite spots to watch a sunset."

"I've never had a sunset picnic in a car before. It sounds fun, doesn't it, Oliver?"

"Yeah. I've never had a picnic in a car either."

Max tilted his head toward the back seat. "I figured sandwiches would be our least messy option."

She smiled at him. "Good call. Thank you."

The evening was clear, with just enough clouds to give the colors something to reflect off, and the sun was already low in the sky. They drove up to a small clearing that had a great view of Sapphire Lake. With the colors spreading across both the clouds above and the lake below, it looked like an artist had carefully painted each stroke.

She took a few pictures of the scene before them, then put her phone down and stared, as if memorizing it. "This is amazing."

Even Oliver's voice held a quiet awe when he said, "The colors in the sky are so cool. I'm going to draw this when I get back to the hotel."

Max pulled the takeout bag from the back seat and offered Ava first choice of the sandwiches. After Max prayed for their dinner, Ava looked over at Zeus. "I can't believe he didn't touch the food."

"It's his training . . . and I gave him his dinner at the station just in case. How was your visit with Colette?"

She broke into a grin. "Well, due to some unfortunate circumstances, Colette is going to have some empty seats at the Thanksgiving table."

"Then why are you smiling—wait, did she convince you to take two of those empty seats?"

She nodded. "She was so concerned when she found out that her son and daughter-in-law had to leave town suddenly that I couldn't say no."

"Well, hallelujah. Colette can be quite persuasive. Is everything okay, though? Why do Jack and Amanda have to leave town?"

He watched her as she answered, but she gave no hint of a connection to Jack. "Her father fell off a ladder trying to put up Christmas lights. He apparently insists that he's fine, but they wanted to go check on him to make sure."

"Makes sense. They're good people, Jack and Amanda."

She suddenly studied her sandwich intently. "I haven't met them, but they sound nice. Since Amanda was going to be making pies tomorrow, we're going to help Colette and Kara make them." At the mention of Colette and Kara, her eyes glistened.

Oliver reached over and put his hand on Zeus's head. "Did you hear that, Zeus? We're gonna stay longer!"

Max couldn't stop his grin. "It sounds like I'm not the only one who wants you to stay."

"It looks like we're all getting our wish. Amanda was going to help Colette with the store on Black Friday and this weekend, so I told Colette I would help her in the shop for as long as she needs." She smiled. "We're not leaving quite yet."

"And Miss Colette said I can draw special pictures for her customers. I'm gonna start them tonight. People will like my trees."

Ava beamed at her son. "Yes, Miss Colette is very excited to have an Artist in Residence for a day or two."

"You're going to help for as long as she needs, huh?" His chest nearly exploded. She was staying. His face warmed when they shared a smile. "It's a Thanksgiving miracle."

"Yes, it is."

He reached across the console and took her hand. "I'll be sure to let God know how thankful I am to spend the holiday with you."

"I am too."

Oliver piped up from the back seat. "Me too. Can we make a snowman now?"

"Sure."

When they all piled out of the car and made a snowman, he felt like he had stepped into someone else's life—someone else's family. And he wanted it to be his.

The sunset exceeded all expectations, and Max and Ava sat talking long after Oliver and Zeus fell asleep in the backseat. It was easy talking with her, and they didn't lack for topics.

She listened intently and asked all the right questions when he told her about his parents and brother, and she told him more about her mother and the close friends she had in Florida. When he talked about the differences between being a cop in the city and a small town and what a hard adjustment it was when he moved to Lakes End, she held his hand and drew out more than he had intended to share. She glowed when she talked about her store and how much she loved serving people there and helping them find the perfect items. He comforted her when she talked about losing her business and home in the hurricane.

They talked about everything. Everything except what had brought each of them to Summit County.

Chapter 23

AVA WOKE EARLY THE next morning and immediately wrote down everything she could remember from her time with Colette and Kara. She was glad that she had bought a new notepad while she was at Up North Clothing and Treasures, because she had a lot more information to write down after their afternoon together. She'd learned enough about her half brothers to feel like she knew them and enough about Kara to wish they could be real sisters.

Instead of fighting the thoughts about Max, she started writing about him too. Like the details about her family, the ones about him were also going to have to last a lifetime. She had tried to come up with a way to have a future with him, but didn't see how she could do that without risking the truth coming out and disrupting Jack's family's life.

She called Sarita while Oliver was in the bathroom. She answered almost immediately. "I got your text last night. You're really staying for a while?"

Ava's stomach leaped. "Yes, and we're spending Thanksgiving with my grandmother, brothers and sister, and even with Max."

"This is such an answer to prayer. I've been asking God to make you stay."

She affected a pouting voice. "You don't want us to come home?"

Sarita laughed. "Very funny. You know I miss you, but I don't think you're done there—especially if you were out stargazing with Max last night."

Ava's cheeks warmed as she pictured his face with the last golden rays of daylight on it. "It was amazing."

"The stars were or he was?"

"A little bit of both." She twisted her ring. "It's going to be hard to leave him."

Sarita paused. "Then don't."

She made it sound so easy. "You know I can't stay here. I won't do that to Jack or his family."

"If they're such nice people, they may welcome you into the family, or at least be cordial."

"I can't risk it. I won't hurt Colette or Jack that way."

"Enrique and I talked about it last night, and he thinks he would want to know if there was a child walking around with his DNA." Enrique was a quiet man and a deep thinker. He would have given a lot of thought before giving his answer to such a question.

"Well, Jack seems to be a good guy, but I'm not so sure that he would welcome the intrusion."

She looked at the clock. "I've got to get Oliver ready and get out the door. I can't believe we're going to bake pies with my grandmother and my sister."

"Don't overthink it, Ava. Enjoy the time you have with her, and ask God if He wants you to tell them who you really are."

Ava palmed her face. "I'm embarrassed to say that as much as I've prayed about this situation, I haven't asked Him that."

Sarita chuckled. "Well, I have. I've prayed about every detail of this trip, and I don't believe for a second that it's a coincidence that you met Max or Colette—or even that you saw Jack."

"As much as I want that to be true, I didn't come to disrupt anything."

She braced herself for whatever was coming when she heard Sarita inhale. "I know you have to go make pies, but I want you to think about something, okay?"

"Okay." She held her breath and squeezed her eyes shut.

"You put your life on hold for years so you could be there for your mom. It's your turn to live now."

Her shoulders relaxed when she let the words sink in. "Thanks, Sarita. I needed to hear that today."

When she pulled up in front of Colette's well-maintained Craftsman, she was overcome by emotion. *I'm at my grandmother's house.* While Oliver gathered his things in the back seat, she snapped a few pictures of the house to remember it by.

She had all afternoon to store memories for both herself and her son. She was going to make the most of it.

Ava looked up as Colette opened the front door and waved. She didn't know what God's plan was for her trip, but she was going to cherish every moment with Colette today. Kara wouldn't be arriving for another hour, so it would be just the three of them at first. *Show me, Lord. If I'm supposed to tell them who I am, please make it clear.*

Once inside, Ava took in every sight and smell. The house was old and creaky, but its character won her over immediately. Colette gave them a tour, and she saw the bedrooms that Jack and his brother occupied as children. Colette had redone the bedrooms for her grandchildren, and as she told stories, it was easy to picture the house full of love and laughter.

It was a stark contrast to her own upbringing. There was plenty of love, but none of the noise and happy chaos Colette described. With only her mother and herself, there was more than enough room to spread out in their high-rise condo in Miami Beach. Everything had its place, and when her mother entertained colleagues or peers she volunteered with, they all raved about her eye for elegant and minimalistic interior design.

Colette's home, with family pictures and mementos everywhere, was much more in line with Ava's style. She didn't like clutter, but she loved to be surrounded by things that had history and carried memories. "This is possibly the warmest home I've ever been in."

Colette beamed as she looked at the pictures that filled the wall, telling the story of a family. "We were very happy here. Now it feels a little big and empty sometimes, but the memories keep me company."

In the small kitchen, Colette had set out all of the ingredients they would need for the pies. Ava pulled out her phone and took a picture of the counter. "Before picture."

Oliver tugged on her arm. "Let's take a picture of us before we get messy."

Colette smiled. "That's a wonderful idea, Oliver. Then we'll take an after picture with all the pies we're going to make."

"I can't wait." Ava held out the phone for a selfie with her son and her grandmother, hoping Colette didn't see the moisture in her eyes. "Now put us to work."

Colette did. Ava didn't have much experience with baking and always took the safe route of visiting bakeries for her desserts, so she offered to do non-baking tasks and clean up behind Colette. She even brought out Oliver's drawing supplies. The woman wouldn't hear of it and gave both her and Oliver simple instructions to start with.

When Oliver stood on Colette's stool, he was the perfect height for her to hold her hands over his and show him what to do. Ava took several videos of Colette patiently teaching and Oliver following all her instructions. She would keep them forever.

Ava's skill and confidence grew with each slice of an apple and measure of a dry ingredient. Learning along with her son at her grandmother's side was like a dream come true. By the time Kara arrived, Ava and Oliver had each successfully made a pie crust under Colette's careful guidance. They also wore as much flour as they put into the bowls.

Kara congratulated them on a job well done. "Grandma is the best teacher, isn't she?"

"Absolutely."

Colette's eyes softened when she looked at her granddaughter. "Kara has been one of my best students. All that's needed is time and patience to learn."

Kara giggled. "How did I ever learn then?" Ava didn't get the inside joke, but Kara explained, "I'm not exactly known for being patient."

"That's one way of putting it." Colette gave Kara's arm a loving squeeze. "Thank you all for helping me today. It's so much more fun to do it together."

Oliver held his flour-encrusted hands up. "Wait! We need a messy picture."

"You're right." Ava held the phone out to capture the four of them.

The desire to pretend for a moment that the secret was out and they were spending the day as a family was strong. Ava cleaned Oliver up, then excused herself to the restroom to get back into reality. While there, she pulled the blank recipe cards and pen Colette had given her from the back pocket of her jeans. It would only take a minute to write down what she had learned during their time together. Every moment and detail were so precious that she was afraid she might forget something if she waited until later.

On the way back to the kitchen, she tucked the cards into her purse for safekeeping. The smells from the kitchen had filled the whole house, and she inhaled deeply as she walked, hoping the memory of it would seal into her mind.

When she walked back into the kitchen, her heart almost burst at the sight. Kara was holding out her phone and taking more pictures in front of the pies with Oliver and Colette. Oliver's giggle held such joy. Ava prayed that he would remember this day forever.

Kara handed Ava her phone. "If you'll put your number in, I'll text the pictures to you."

"Thanks!" She tried not to let her fingers shake as she typed in the numbers. As silly as it was, it felt like a real connection.

Ava looked at all of the crusts that were gathering on the kitchen table. "Will all of these pies get eaten with the smaller crowd?"

Colette laughed. "These aren't only for tomorrow's dinner. One apple pie is for Vernon and Maxwell to take home and the extra chocolate and pumpkin are for Sunday when we go pick out the Christmas tree."

What she wouldn't give to be a part of family Christmas tree picking. Reality hit her, and the fantasy of being a part of the Sullivan family blew away like the steam from the pot on the stove.

Kara laid a comforting hand on her back. "I'm sorry. You must miss your mom terribly right now."

Ava thanked God for the easy explanation for her sudden mood change. "I do. This Christmas will be a very different experience for me. Thank you both for including me for Thanksgiving."

Colette wrapped her sweet, grandmotherly arms around Ava's shoulders. "This Thanksgiving, we're your family."

Chapter 24

MAX TOOK THE FASTEST shower of his life when he got done with work on Thanksgiving. He set the cruise control on his car so that he wouldn't break land speed records to get to Colette's house. The celebration had started hours ago, and he wanted to enjoy as much of the day as possible before everyone went home in turkey comas.

A few inches of snow had fallen to the ground, so Gramps had picked Ava and Oliver up at the hotel, giving Max the excuse to drive them home later. She had resisted the idea at first, but he told her that Gramps wanted to make sure she got there safely. He had given her another driving lesson last night after dinner, but even though she was getting the hang of winter driving, she was still not confident. Scared drivers made mistakes, and Max wanted her to be able to handle the drive through Michigan and Ohio on her way home when she left. He tried not to think of the limited time he had with her as he parked on the street in front of Colette's house.

Walking in, he was greeted by the sound of happy conversation and the smell of turkey, stuffing, and all the traditional Thanksgiving dishes that were being passed around the table. Gramps was at the head of the table carving the turkey, and Jack's three children were passing food around. The rest of Colette's family would be there for Christmas, so the Thanksgiving gathering was modest.

Colette winked as she pointed out the empty seat next to Ava after welcoming him with a hug. "You're right on time, Maxwell. Everyone just sat down."

"You didn't have to hold dinner off for me."

"I know I didn't, but everyone wanted to. We knew you would be here any minute, and we just sat down. Your grandpa hasn't even prayed yet."

He kissed her on the cheek. "I appreciate it. You gave me another thing to be thankful for." With his job, it was rare to get holidays off, and he often had to either leave before the meal started or heat up leftovers when he got to wherever they were gathering. He much preferred the latter, and working the day shift meant that he didn't have to go on the domestic disturbance complaints that happened all too often on holiday evenings when families who didn't get along spent the day together. It was a special treat to enjoy the meal with the group, especially the captivating woman next to him.

He leaned over to whisper in Ava's ear. "You look extra beautiful today."

"Thank you."

His heart skipped a beat when her cheeks pinked at his compliment, so he decided to double down. "I can't wait to taste the pies you and Oliver made."

"Me too!" She had looked almost giddy when she had talked about her baking lesson with Colette and Kara last night over dinner, and it was no different today.

Oliver peeked around his mother. "Me three!"

"They were great students." Colette smiled proudly at her new protégées.

Kara tickled Oliver. "Agreed. They both picked it up faster than I did, and Oliver made an entire new outfit out of flour."

The boy giggled at her teasing. "Miss Colette said good cooks make messes."

Gramps sat down after expertly slicing the turkey and led the group in prayer. His prayers had always left Max feeling like he had just left a short and powerful church service.

Ava whispered, "Wow, that was wonderful."

"He's pretty great, isn't he?"

"You're very fortunate to be able to grow up with a spiritual leader like him in your life."

Max felt a twang of regret. "I wish I would have known it and listened better when I was younger, but yes, I'm very fortunate. Mostly for his prayers when I wasn't following too well."

She gave him a compassionate look. "It would be nice if we had wisdom in the earlier times of our lives, but sometimes we have to learn things the hard way."

Their conversation was interrupted by the turkey platter coming their way. He held it for Ava, then she took it while he loaded his plate.

As the meal went on, he watched Ava listen intently to every story told. Whoever was speaking had her full attention, as if they were the only person in the room.

It was no wonder he was falling for her. She had a light within her and a deep caring for others that he had found to be rare in the world. He needed to find a way to get her to stay, or at least to agree to visit soon. Never a fan of long-distance relationships, he might be willing to give one a try if she was.

Kara started telling a story about one of the clients at the salon earlier in the week. It seemed that the elderly woman thought Kara was so talented at styling hair that she could make her dog look as beautiful as her clients and begged Kara to try. Max and Ava laughed along with everyone else as she described her attempts to transfer styling techniques from humans to a Golden Retriever.

Ava seemed to be enjoying herself, but there was a sadness in her eyes. It had to be hard to be in a room full of people she had just met on the first Thanksgiving without her mother. He silently prayed that God would bless the day for her and give her the comfort that only He could provide.

Ava helped Colette and Kara bring out the pies, ice cream, and coffee while Max and Jack's two sons, J.J. and Travis, cleared the dinner dishes from the table. When they all sat and ate pie, Max decided that he would have a heart-to-heart with Ava on the way home about any possibility for a future together. He wanted more evenings like this, and he wanted Ava to be a part of them.

Kara scooted away from the table to take a phone call. "Hi, Mom . . . Yes, we're just finishing dessert. Did you and Dad decide to come for pie?"

He felt as much as saw Ava stiffen. After his fruitless attempts to find a connection between her and Jack, he had started to convince himself that he was making up what he had seen at the church. The look on her face confirmed that he had indeed seen what he thought he had. She looked trapped as she fidgeted with her napkin. Her brows knitted together in concentration, especially when Kara walked out of hearing distance. He suspected that if Jack was coming to Colette's house, Ava would want to be long gone first.

When Kara came back into the room, she addressed Colette. "Mom and Dad are coming back tomorrow. They said they're sorry and that they'll make it up to you by eating extra pie."

As everyone else at the table laughed, Ava exhaled. She excused herself and walked into the kitchen. Colette followed her with her eyes, then looked at Max. When he excused himself, she smiled and nodded. She had become as attached to Ava in the short time they'd known each other as Ava had her.

Ava was standing on the back porch, shivering in the cold.

"You okay?"

"I just needed some air."

She looked like she was on the verge of tears, and he wrapped his arms around her and pulled her to his chest. "Getting some air here is different than in Florida. You're shivering."

"It's okay." She held him tightly and relaxed against him. "I'm starting to like the cold air."

This feels so right. He kept his thoughts to himself as they stood there. The last thing he wanted to do was scare her away or ruin any time he had left with her. "The pies were extra delicious this year. My compliments to the new chefs."

She smiled as she looked up at him. "I can't believe we made pies with—I can't believe we made pies. Oliver loved it."

"I think you're as quick a study with desserts as you have been with winter driving."

She chuckled. "I just hope I don't need many of those driving skills in a couple of days when I drive south."

He squeezed her and lowered his lips to her ear. "Maybe you should stay a little longer."

"I wish I could."

His heart soared with hope. Maybe her resolve to leave was cracking. She looked up at him and time stood still as they gazed into each other's eyes. Feeling the heat of her nearness, he tightened his hold.

He didn't want to push her too far, so he forced his lips to her forehead instead of letting them go where they wanted. Time stood still, and only the sound of ragged breaths and their heartbeats filled the air. His knees almost buckled when she looked back into his eyes. *Please don't walk away now.*

Instead of stepping away from him, she grabbed the collar of his shirt. When she pressed her lips to his, he forgot about the cold air, the people waiting for them inside, and his own fears. In that moment, he may have forgotten his own name.

He held her tightly as they drank each other in. There was something different in her kiss—in her.

He was done for.

As quickly as she had started the kiss, she broke it.

He locked his arms around her, keeping her heart against his. It took all his strength to push words past the tightness in his throat. "Ava, please let me in."

She dropped her head to his chest. "I can't . . ."

Every fiber of his being told him that she felt everything he did. Then what was holding her back? And what did it have to do with Jack?

"I have to go inside."

He was too spent to stop her when she pushed away from him.

"I'm sorry, Max." She turned and disappeared into the house, taking his every hope and desire with her.

Chapter 25

WHAT HAD SHE JUST done? Ava had never in her life initiated a first kiss with a man. But then, she had never wanted to kiss a man as much as she had wanted to kiss Max Brody.

When he had wrapped his arms around her and pulled her to him, she felt things she had never felt before. His kiss was unlike anything she'd ever known. How was she going to walk away from him for good?

With every second she'd spent in his arms, she had allowed him deeper into her heart. The heat in his eyes had told her the feeling was mutual. How could she have let things get so out of hand? No matter how badly she wanted it, she couldn't have a future with him. She had to keep her secret from him—from everyone—for the good of everyone who had become dear to her over the short time she had been in Michigan.

She rushed to the bathroom. It was as good as any place she had ever used for a prayer closet. "Lord, please help me. This whole trip has been one risk after another, and the more time I spend here, the worse the heartbreak is going to be." She closed her eyes and willed her heart to slow down. "Please just get me through this weekend and let me say goodbye to this place and these wonderful people.

And help me pick up the pieces of my broken heart when I get home."

She washed her hands and face, wishing she could wash away the last twenty minutes. Leaving was going to be hard enough; leaving when she knew just how amazing it was to be in Max's arms and having his lips on hers was going to be pretty near impossible.

Taking a deep breath, she opened the bathroom door. Colette stood in the hallway waiting for her. "Would you come in here for a moment?" She took her by the hand and led her toward her bedroom.

Ava followed, wishing she could share all of her secrets with the sweet woman without upending her entire world.

Colette gestured to the chair as she sat on her bed. "I know the first Thanksgiving without your mom must be very hard. Do you want to stay in here for a few minutes and get your bearings?"

She could only nod. Colette was right. Even if Ava's heart wasn't being pulled in ten different directions, not having her mother there was painful in its own right.

Colette stood and squeezed her shoulder. "Take all the time you need. I'll keep an eye on Oliver."

"You're a wonderful friend, Colette."

"So are you, honey. I'm glad you came today."

Ava leaned back in the soft chair and closed her eyes after Colette left the room. She breathed in the soft scent of perfume that filled the room, wishing she could capture scents on her notes about her family and Max.

When she heard two cars start outside, she jerked awake. How long had she dozed in there? It was getting late, and Colette probably wanted to go to bed soon. Max was supposed to drive them home and, after what happened on the porch, it was good that they would have Oliver there as a chaperone. She didn't trust herself to be alone with Max tonight. His arms, his lips, his very presence were too inviting.

She sighed. *Avoid all temptation. Particularly the heart kind.*

Why hadn't she driven her own car? She sat for a moment, considering her alternatives, and landed on the idea to ask Kara to drive her and Oliver home.

When she walked out into the living room, only Max and Vernon remained. Oliver barely kept his eyes open as he watched them take the leaves out of the dining table and put the furniture back in its proper spot. She hadn't realized how much time had passed when she was in Colette's room, but it looked like she'd missed the bulk of the cleanup.

Colette smiled at her. "Kara and the boys all had to go, but she said to tell you she'll see you at the store tomorrow afternoon."

So much for that plan. "Can I help with dishes?"

"They're all done. I've put some leftovers in containers for all of you, so don't forget them."

Vernon approached her with his coat in his hand. "Good night, Miss Ava. I'm looking forward to my day with Oliver tomorrow while you're working."

Oliver perked up at the mention of his planned day with Vernon. "Me too. I'll be ready to make my snow baseball and do tricks with Zeus and help you cook a yummy dinner."

She was certain that an entire day spent with Vernon and Zeus would be a highlight of Oliver's trip. And she had all day tomorrow to figure out how to spend another evening at Max's home without wanting to claim it—and him—as hers. She definitely needed to come up with a plan to stop herself from kissing him again.

"Oliver and I decided we're going to make Sloppy Joes while you and Maxwell are working. Be sure to bring your appetite."

"I will. Thank you again for offering." If she could come up with a way to enjoy an evening with Max and Vernon without wishing for things she couldn't have, it would be a perfect ending to the day with Colette and would provide ample memories to keep her company when she and Oliver were back in Miami.

Max helped her into her coat and turned to hug their hostess. "Thank you for another wonderful meal, Aunt Colette."

The floor dropped right out from under Ava.

Aunt? Had she planted the most amazing kiss of her life on her cousin?

Chapter 26

MAX FELT THE PRESSURE of the clock as he steered the car away from Colette's house and drove in the direction of Ava's hotel. Oliver fell asleep almost immediately, and Ava quietly looked out the window at the dark night.

He had precious little time to convince her to stay, or at least to consider letting their relationship develop long-distance. That kiss was as full of emotion and hope as it was desire, but she had pulled away and avoided him since. She hadn't said a word since they walked out of the house.

"Do you want to talk about it?"

She kept her head turned toward the window. "There isn't anything to talk about." Her voice was quiet, and she sounded sad, maybe even lost.

His gut clenched. He was losing her.

When he reached for her hand, she pulled it away and leaned closer to her door.

"You have a lot on your mind. Do you want to talk about any of it?"

"No. It's been a long day, and I'm tired."

This was worse than when he was trying to get information out of her when she first got to town. At least then she engaged. When he turned onto the two-lane highway that led to Lakes End and her hotel, he could almost hear a clock ticking in his head. "What's going to happen when you leave?"

She finally looked at him. "What do you mean?"

"Are you going to just forget all of this? Forget us?"

"There can't be an us, Max." She turned back to the window.

"Your lips told a different story earlier."

"That was a mistake. I'm sorry."

His gut absorbed her sucker punch. *A mistake.*

"Is that because of Jack Sullivan?"

She inhaled sharply and her head jerked in his direction. Her eyes darted around the car, as if she would find her response in there somewhere. "I don't know Jack Sullivan."

"Then why do you react like that when you hear his name? I'm not buying it, Ava. If he's giving you some kind of trouble, I can help you."

"I don't know what you're talking about."

He wanted to pull over to talk, to give them more time. The way she was clinging to the door, she would probably open it and run. He needed to change tactics.

"Okay, I'll talk then." He was grasping at straws, but he had to do something. "We've had an amazing time together and gotten to know each other since the day you crashed into my life. I've never felt the way I feel when I'm with you."

"Max, please don't." She wiped a tear from her eye.

"I know you feel the same, but what I don't know is why you're denying it."

She sat quietly, sniffling.

"Ava . . . give us a chance."

She didn't respond, but the tears she was so clearly and valiantly fighting spoke for her. Silence filled the car like a heavy fog.

He had never hated a building as much as he hated the hotel that was looming closer. Turning into the parking lot took everything in him.

When he stopped in front of the door, he jumped out of the car before she could grab Oliver and bolt. He got to her side before she stood, and when he wrapped his arms around her, she clung tightly to him.

Just when he started to hope that he hadn't lost her yet, she stepped away and opened the back door.

"I've got him." He gently nudged her aside and unbuckled Oliver, then carried him toward the lobby door. She followed with the booster seat, then led Max wordlessly to their room. With every step they took, the hole in his chest grew.

She avoided eye contact while Max settled Oliver onto his bed. When he turned around, she was holding the door open.

"Ava—"

She still wouldn't look at him. "Good night, Max."

When he got home, Zeus was waiting. Max changed clothes and took the dog for a run. He wasn't sure who needed it more at that moment, but he was thankful for the companionship.

The cold air on his face and hard ground beneath his feet were the only things keeping him from feeling like he was spinning out of control in the dark night. What was keeping Ava from him? And why did he care so much?

Zeus kept time with him as his feet moved faster and faster. The dog's injury had healed enough that he had no limitations, and Max knew without a doubt that God had used the injury to give him a trusted companion after what he had gone through in Flint.

Max's thoughts flew as quickly as his feet. How had Ava burrowed her way into his heart so quickly? When he had woken up in that Flint hospital room five years ago, his trust in humanity, God, and himself was gone. He trusted only his parents, his brother, his grandpa, and Zeus. It took a while to let others in again. When he moved to Lakes End, his trust in God, people he'd known throughout his life, and himself started to trickle back. He had to risk trusting Wyatt because they were partners and had to have each other's backs on calls.

When had he started to trust Ava? He wasn't sure when or even how it had happened, only that it had. Now that she was in his protected inner circle, he wanted her to stay there. Watching her distance herself tonight—first on Colette's porch and then at the hotel—had been brutal. He would do anything to make sure that didn't happen again. His moves over the next few days would make or break his chance at a life with her.

He slowed himself to a halt. Zeus watched him, waiting for his next signal. Spreading his arms wide, Max looked at the sky. "It looks like I need another miracle, Lord. You gave me Zeus and saved Gramps from the heart attack that could have taken him. You gave me a new life here even after I messed up so badly in Flint. I know I may be being greedy in asking for Ava too, but please help."

Chapter 27

AVA FELT DRUGGED THE next morning and was thankful that Oliver had slept later than usual. Shoving any and all thoughts of Max firmly aside, she focused on filling her notebook with everything she wanted to remember about her family while she drank her morning tea.

The Sullivans were a boisterous group, nothing like she was used to. The easy camaraderie Jack's children shared seemed so natural and comfortable. Even Max seemed to know most of the inside jokes. She almost tore up the notes about Max, then realized he might belong in the other group—the family group. *Could Max really be my family?*

She went back through her notes. He had told her the families were close, especially his mother and Colette, but he had never said they were related. Were the two women sisters? She begged God for answers, for some way for it not to be true, but none came.

When Oliver finished his breakfast, she put the notebook down. Her hand hurt from writing so fast in the small amount of time she'd had, but she didn't want to forget a detail.

Oliver brushed his teeth quickly and pulled his coat and boots on. "Come on, Mom. I don't want to be late." *Like mother, like son.*

"You won't be late." She took her time getting to the car, hoping Max would be gone when she dropped Oliver off. Looking into his eyes would only hurt. "You're pretty excited to play with Mr. Vernon today, huh?"

"And Zeus. I get to help Mr. Vernon do drills and I'm going to teach him a new trick."

To Ava's relief, Max's car was gone when they arrived at the house. After the way she'd acted last night, he was probably hoping to miss her too. Vernon and Zeus were in the yard waiting, and Oliver ran to join them. Her son barely looked in her direction when she said goodbye.

During the short drive to Up North Clothing and Treasures, she begged God to help her to relax and enjoy the time she had with Colette and Kara. Thinking about Max and what she couldn't have only hurt, and she needed to focus on making memories while she had the chance.

She wished she had declined Vernon's invitation to stay for dinner when she picked Oliver up. How was she supposed to act natural if she was sitting across the table from the man of her dreams who, through some cruel twist of fate, was her cousin?

When she arrived at the store, Colette had everything ready for her customers. The station she set up with coffee, tea, and cider gave the place a welcoming and festive scent that went well with the Christmas music playing. "Good morning! Thank you again for helping me out today."

"I'm happy to help, and working with your customers helps me miss mine less." *Also, you're my grandmother, and I would do anything to spend time with you.*

The morning wasn't too busy, but by eleven, everyone who had gone to Traverse City for the early sales was back to support the local merchants. Ava and Colette worked well together, and Kara came to help out for a few hours as well. The time with them felt like an extra blessing, especially because it gave her little time to think about Max or the mess she'd made with him.

By two o'clock, Colette looked like she was ready to drop. The crowd had thinned out, so Ava offered to manage the store on her own and let her go home for a rest.

Colette laughed as she filled the hot water kettle. "Nothing a little tea and a snack won't fix." She searched the drawers in the small accent table she used to store tea bags. "I'm not going to take a nap, but I will run home to fetch us some more tea. Are you sure you don't mind watching the store for a little while?"

"Not at all. Take your time."

When she left, Ava pulled out the recipe cards she'd been using to write down facts and memories. There were a few tidbits she had learned from Colette and Kara, so she jotted them down while she had a moment then stuck them back into her purse.

The door jingled, and Ava looked up, expecting a customer. Instead, she was face-to-face with Jack Sullivan.

Her mouth went dry. Should she act like she knew him, or pretend she had no idea who he was and try to get rid of him? As much as she wanted to know him, the latter was best for everyone.

Help me move into shopkeeper mode, Lord. "Good afternoon. Can I help you find something?"

His brows furrowed as he looked around the store. "Is Colette around? I'm her son."

She feigned surprise. "Oh! I'm sorry, she just ran home for something. You can probably catch her there." *Please leave. I'm not here to mess up your life.*

He gave a warm smile. "If she's coming right back, I'll wait."

She turned her head to hide her wince. "Sure, no problem." Ava busied herself with organizing gift bags and boxes at the counter and trying to keep her breathing and heart rate normal.

"She didn't mention she'd hired help." He walked to the counter and stretched his hand out to her. "I'm Jack Sullivan."

Her heart raced more as she shook his hand. "It's nice to meet you . . . Jack." She cleared her dry throat. "Ava Barton. I'm helping Colette out today."

He grinned. "Ah, you're the Ava I've been hearing about."

Lord, please send a customer in here—anything to get me out of this conversation. "I'm just here for a few days."

"Well, I don't know how you convinced my mother to accept help today, but thank you." His warm smile and friendly tone were a lot like Colette's. She allowed herself a moment to study his features. If only she could spend a few minutes getting to know him.

She knew danger when she saw it, though, and talking to him was definitely dangerous. So was wishing for a father.

Maybe if she could get away from him for a few minutes, Colette would get back. "Actually, Jack, since you're here, would you mind watching the store so I can take a quick bathroom break?"

"Sure, go ahead."

She grabbed her purse and forced herself to walk casually toward the back of the store.

"Wait a minute. You dropped something." He bent down to pick up something from the floor.

Her lungs seized. It was one of the recipe cards.

No! Please don't look at it, please don't look at it.

As he strode across the room to hand it to her, he glanced down at the card. He stopped dead in his tracks and stared at it, reading the notes she had so carefully taken.

His jaw tensed as he cocked his head. "Do you mind telling me why you've been taking notes on my family?" His eyes zeroed in on her with a laser-like focus. The friendly sparkle of a moment ago was replaced by suspicion.

She stared at him, silenced by her own panic and guilt. "I'm sorry, I—"

"You what?"

What could she possibly say to get out of this?

He took a step forward. "I'd like an explanation."

She looked down, staring a hole in the floor. "I . . . I was just curious."

"About what?" His brows lowered. "Do I need to call the police?"

"No!" She didn't know what to do. Dishonesty made her squeamish, and she had never been able to think fast on her feet. "I'm sorry, Jack. I never meant to cause any trouble."

He folded his arms across his chest. He was apparently not a man who was going to put up with getting the runaround, and now he thought she was stalking his family. She could see the concern in his eyes. His children's names were on that card, as were a myriad of personal details about them.

As much as she didn't want to tell him the truth, she also didn't want him to think that his family was in any kind of jeopardy. "I was only curious."

"Curious about what? Why are you so curious about my family— my children?"

He reached for his phone.

"No, Jack. I—" She gulped. There was no way out. She had no choice but to tell him.

"Wait." Taking a deep breath, she forced herself to speak. "Does the Westside Cryobank sound familiar to you?"

He furrowed his brow. "It doesn't ring a bell. Should it?"

"Yes—no. It was a long time ago." She reached for the water bottle she had left on the counter and took a shaky sip. "It was in

Ann Arbor, not far from the University of Michigan campus."

"Not following."

"It was, um—" She lowered her eyes again, embarrassed at the topic. "It was a tissue bank."

He sighed. "Why would you ask about—" He took a step back and his hand flew to his mouth.

Either the room went silent or Ava went deaf. Her pulse pounded in her ears. She spoke the obvious. "I'm the outcome of your donation."

Jack rubbed his jaw as he studied her face. "You're telling me you're my daughter?"

She flushed at the scrutiny as she nodded. "Biologically, anyway."

"What are you here for?"

She swallowed, blinking back tears. "I'm not really sure. I was curious when my mother died. I didn't have family, and I wondered about you."

He took a couple of steps away and stared at the back wall. She was frozen in place, watching him.

His eyes burned into her when he turned back around. "So you came here, what, to study me? To have a family reunion?"

"It was research, I guess." She cursed her curiosity. "I just thought maybe if I saw what you looked like, I would have some sort of closure. When I met Colette, I had no idea she was your mother, but we became friends immediately."

"And?"

"And?"

He looked down at the card. "Were you here for something else? Did you—what do you want with my family?"

"Nothing. It was just curiosity."

"Have you gotten the information you want?" He looked at the recipe card, as if debating what to do with it. "Is your curiosity satisfied?"

She nodded. "Yes." Her voice was barely a whisper.

Her panic rose as they stood there avoiding each other's eyes.

"I don't know what to tell you . . ." He took slow steps forward and handed the card to her.

She carefully took it from his hand, her own shaking. "I'm sorry, Jack, I didn't mean to cause trouble."

Time stopped as he stared at her. Wishing she could disappear, she turned and scurried out of the shop and into the cold wind.

Chapter 28

MAX WALKED OUT OF the drugstore with a prescription for Gramps in his pocket. He thought about walking down to Colette's store, but he didn't want to push his luck with Ava today. As far as he knew, she was still going to come to dinner tonight. That would give him one last chance. Hopefully.

Seeing a blur of motion out of the corner of his eye, he turned as she came running down the street without a coat on. She was looking at the ground instead of at the post she was on a collision course with, so he stepped in front of it just in time to catch her in his arms. "Whoa—are you alright?"

She gasped when he grabbed her. "Max!"

He looked up to see Jack step from the doorway of Colette's store. Immediately his chest hardened. "Did he do something to you?" Friend or not, he would tear the guy's head off if he hurt her.

Jack looked her over without acknowledging Max and walked back into the store.

When she quivered in his arms, he tightened his grip. "It's okay, I'm not going to let anyone hurt you."

She shook her head. "No one is hurting me." Her tears told a different story. He turned around, taking her with him, and guided her toward his car. When he opened the door, she sat in the passenger seat without a word.

"Where's your coat?"

"I left it at Colette's shop."

"You stay here. I'll be right back." He handed her his key fob. "Take this and turn the heat on." She barely nodded as she took it.

On the short walk to Colette's store, he worked to settle himself down. He wouldn't get information from anyone if he went in with fists flying, but he was going to get information. He'd had it with the mystery of what was between Ava and Jack.

When he stormed through the door, Jack looked as shaken as Ava had. He cleared his throat. "Is she okay?"

Max nailed him with a look. *She's nowhere close.* "What just happened here?"

Jack scratched his jaw. "She didn't tell you?"

Max answered with a silent glare.

Jack clearly read the answer Max was not giving and straightened his shoulders. "Then I'm not sure that's any of your business."

"Ava is my business." Max took a step toward him. "Jack, if you hurt her . . ."

Jack stepped around him but offered no answer.

"What did you do to her?"

Jack gave him a hard look. "I didn't do a thing."

Jack didn't look right. He looked like he had just been told that someone died. Once again, the evidence wasn't adding up to anything.

Colette walked in from the back room with her usual smile. "Jack—oh good, you met—" She looked around the store. "Where did Ava go?"

Jack gave Max a look of warning. "She wasn't feeling well and had to leave."

Colette frowned. "Oh, the poor dear. She's been having such a hard time without her mother this Thanksgiving. I knew something was wrong today, but she didn't tell me she was sick." She looked at Max. "Maxwell, it's good to see you."

He forced a smile for her benefit. No need to drag her into it. "I came for Ava's coat. She left it behind."

"Oh, I'll get it."

When she slipped into the back room, Max took a step closer to Jack and lowered his voice. "This conversation is not over."

Without a word, Jack spun and walked into the back room himself.

Collette returned and handed Max the coat. "Please tell her I'm praying for her."

"I will."

"Tell her I'll call her later, and if she doesn't feel up to helping me out tomorrow, it's okay. Amanda will be here."

He nodded and kissed her on the cheek. "I'll pass that on to her."

As Max turned to walk out the door, Collette laid a hand on his arm. "Maxwell, take care of her."

He smiled. "I'll do my best."

When he got to his car, Ava sat as still as a statue and was staring at what looked like an index card. She quickly tucked whatever it was into her purse and wiped her eyes when he got into his seat.

He wanted to get her as far away from Jack as he could. He didn't need to know the details to know that the man upset her.

"Thank you, Max." Her voice was barely audible.

"I told you I'd like to help you, that I would do anything I could."

She nodded. "I know."

"The problem is, I don't know what to do to help you."

She nodded again. "I know. I owe you an explanation."

"You don't owe me anything, but I would like to know what has you so rattled." He started out of the parking spot. "Can I take you for a drive?"

"Sure." She finally spared him a look. "Actually, can we go to the beach? The ocean always calms me. Maybe the lake will too."

"Okay." He drove to the end of the street and parked in the beach lot. Thinking it best to give her a moment, and needing one himself, he sat quietly.

She seemed to be collecting herself as she stared out at the angry waves crashing over the breakwater. *Lord, please help her.*

Her eyes remained focused on the lake. "Jack Sullivan is my biological father."

Max let out a breath, both shock and relief flowing with it. He thought back to what he knew about her mother and her age. He had a hard time imagining Jack as a young man having an affair with a woman who was as old as his own mother.

Ava remained silent.

"Not what I expected to hear."

"I never meant for any of this to happen. I just wanted to see a glimpse of him, maybe watch him for a few moments from across a street." She turned to him, her eyes welling up with tears. "I didn't want him to know who I was. I didn't come here to blow up his life."

"That's why you looked so afraid when you saw him."

"I didn't come to town to meet him or his family. I didn't know Collette was his mother when I met her. I just knew she was a wonderful woman I liked to spend time around."

He sighed. "That day at the church . . ."

She nodded. "That's when I realized it."

"Does he know?"

"He does now." She pulled the card out of her purse and handed it to Max. "This fell out of my purse and he saw it. I've been writing down everything that I've learned about his family to give myself something to hold on to when I go back home."

He looked at the card full of anecdotes, descriptions and characteristics of Jack's children. He flipped the card to look at the back. "You don't have anything about Colette or Jack on here."

She reached into her purse and held up three more cards, all equally full of tiny writing.

"So you accidentally saw him and you were going to get out of town before you could meet him."

She nodded. "I didn't want to interrupt anything or risk someone seeing the resemblance and putting two and two together."

"And when you stayed the extra days?"

"That was me being selfish." She closed her eyes and leaned against the headrest. "He went out of town, so I took advantage of the chance to spend more time with Colette and Kara . . . and you. I never should have . . ." Her voice trailed off. It was clear that she was racked with guilt.

He reached over and took her hand. "It's natural to be curious, especially after losing your mother." He tried to wrap his head around the upstanding Jack Sullivan getting involved with an older woman and leaving a child behind that he took no responsibility for. "Jack's not quite the man I thought he was."

Her head snapped up. "No, it wasn't like that. He never knew my mother."

"How—"

She took a deep breath. "When my mother turned forty, she was depressed, lonely . . . She had been an only child and her parents were older when they had her. She had always wanted a family, but she had been focused on her career. By the time she was ready to settle down, she hadn't found anyone to settle down with, so she went to a clinic and purchased a vial from a young donor . . . I was her last chance at motherhood."

"She went to a sperm bank?"

Her eyes searched his. "Yes. It was her last-ditch effort. When she found out she was pregnant, the reality that she had created a fatherless child and become a single mother hit her. She knew that people would look at her askance for being so desperate—and might look at me as an oddity—if they knew the truth, so she packed her bags, changed her name and history, and moved to Florida."

"She changed her name?"

"It made the story about my supposed father dying before I was born more plausible."

"Ahh, she thought of everything."

Ava nodded. "She thought of everything. I grew up believing that my father was her husband who died heroically while saving her from a burning house."

Max's chin dropped to his chest. "Burning house . . . no pictures of him."

"Nope. Everything lost in the fire."

She covered everything but the little girl thrown into the middle of it. "If she covered her tracks so thoroughly, how did you find out the truth?"

Ava gazed back at the water. "When I was eighteen years old, she sat me down and told me. She didn't have much information about him, and I didn't really care to know. I was too busy trying to live up to everything she had sacrificed in order to be a mother to me. But when she died, I was lost."

No wonder Ava carried the world on her shoulders. "How did you find him? I thought those things were private."

"They are. They only give out non-identifying information." She almost smiled. "Kara led me to him."

"Kara?"

"I joined all the websites with the DNA databases, hoping that I would find something about where I came from. I knew it was a long shot, but thought that if some of the holes were filled in about my history, I might feel less like Oliver and I were alone."

"And how does Kara play into this?"

"She was a member of GenealogyWeb, and her privacy settings were such that when I got the notification about a connection, her name was attached to it. An hour of internet searching led me to Hideaway, Michigan."

He reached out and pulled her into his arms. "I'm so sorry."

"Thank you for being such a good friend to me, Max. It's been lonely to have this secret."

"Your secret is safe with me. I assume Colette doesn't know?"

She shook her head. "That will be up to Jack. I only told him because he thought I was stalking his family when he saw the card. I could see the worry on his face, and I didn't want any of that."

"So what now? You were pretty upset when I saw you on the street."

"My grand plan to not cross his path was shattered, and he's not exactly looking to grow his family, so I guess that's that. Time to get out of his town and go home."

Chapter 29

AVA'S STOMACH CHURNED AT least as much as the waves crashing over the breakwater. Max's arms were comforting, even though she knew that nothing could ever be between them. Regardless of any attraction she'd felt, he had been a good friend to her since she got into town. He had gone above and beyond the call of duty every step of the way.

She sat back in her seat. "I just hope I haven't ruined anything."

"Despite what I thought about Jack when I saw you rushing out of Colette's store, he's a good man. I hope you can take some comfort in that."

She nodded, resigned to hold onto whatever little pieces of information she had. "As odd as that is, it does give me comfort. I know I'll never have a relationship with him or his family, but it does help to know that they are wonderful people—all of you are."

All of her family. Max was her family. That idea did nothing to settle her stomach.

He smiled at her sweetly. "So are you. Sounds like maybe you got that from both of your parents."

"I keep thinking about my mother and what she would say about me making this trip. I'm not sure she would think it was such a good idea."

He looked as though he went to a far-off place. "Sometimes we do crazy things when we need answers."

She sighed, wishing the knot would leave her stomach. "Sometimes we do things that get us into big trouble and we need more answers than we realized."

"That's true." He looked back at her. "And like I told you before, I'd like to help you if there's anything I can do. I'm not sure what that would look like now that you don't need my impeccable law enforcement skills, but I'm here for you."

She laughed and wiped her eyes. "Your impeccable friend skills have made all the difference on this trip, especially today. Thank you for being here for me." She closed her eyes. "Now I'm exhausted."

His warm voice filled her ears. "I'll bet you are. You've had quite the trip here. Did you get all your questions answered?"

"No, but I think I got everything I'm going to get answered." She held up the index cards. "Jack didn't exactly invite me for family dinner and history night."

"I wish he would, for what it's worth."

"No, it's okay. He doesn't owe me anything. I owed him the good sense to stay away and not disrupt his life or let him know about my existence, but . . ."

"Well, I can't speak for him, but I would imagine if Jack knew you, he would be pretty proud of you. You're a strong and caring woman, and look at how much you've helped Colette this week."

Tears rushed to her eyes. She had never processed so many emotions at once.

He put his arm around her again. "I'm sorry, I didn't mean to—"

"It's okay. I hate having to leave her . . . Would you take care of her when I'm gone?"

"It would be my honor." He cleared his throat. "Can I ask another question?"

"Sure." She sat back and dug through her purse for her spare tissue pack. "I have no secrets anymore."

"You said you and Oliver were alone, and he said he doesn't have a dad. Is his father not involved?"

She hadn't realized that she'd never told Max the story of her marriage. It seemed like they'd shared their whole histories over the short time they'd known each other. "Elliott died in a car accident on the A1A when Oliver was six months old. He didn't have family either." She dabbed at her swollen eyes. "My mother always felt like she jinxed me, as if lying about being widowed caused me to suffer the same fate."

"I'm sorry—for you and for Oliver." He covered her hand with his. "Is that why you're afraid to get involved? Do you feel like you're betraying his memory?"

Guilt hit again. She never felt like she grieved as much as a wife should have for Elliott, and Max's presence in her life had shown her why. "No. He would want me to be happy and would want Oliver to have a father. I just . . ."

What was she supposed to say? That since she had been in Michigan it didn't feel quite so much like she and Oliver were alone?

He squeezed her hand. "I didn't mean to add on to your burden today. You don't have to talk about him if you're not comfortable."

"It's not that. You know why I resisted getting involved. I can't stay in Jack's town." Thank God she found out they were related before she let her feelings go any further.

"Now that you're not worried about him finding out who you are . . . would you consider staying longer?"

"Oh, Max . . . I think I've done quite enough here."

Chapter 30

MAX SET ANOTHER LOG on the fire, careful not to wake Ava. She had practically passed out the minute she sat on the couch when they returned from the beach. Oliver and Gramps were outside putting the final touches on the snow baseball they had made, and Oliver had asked Max to keep Ava from looking until it was perfect.

After covering her with a blanket and putting a pillow under her head, he tiptoed into the kitchen.

Gramps walked in through the back door. With a nod toward the living room, he kept his voice hushed. "Is she okay?"

He nodded. "She will be. She's had a rough day." Max didn't offer details, and he was thankful that Gramps wasn't one to pry.

The old man glanced out into the living room. "Zeus seems to know she's had a hard time of it. Look at him, standing guard."

Max looked around the corner. The dog sat where he had a view of both Ava and Max and scanned the area, unblinking.

Gramps whispered, "I was going to offer to take him out for drills, but he looks pretty content with his job right now."

"Thanks. I'll wait until after dinner." Max started gathering place settings quietly, needing something to do while he prayed about everything she had told him at the beach.

Lord, please give her peace. Remind her that You were with her when she was talking with Jack today. You've been with her every day of her life. Despite what she's thought about her earthly father, remind her that her heavenly One was there with her every second.

He exhaled and squeezed his eyes shut. *Help her to see what to do next and not to make any rash moves.*

When he walked into the living room, he glimpsed Gramps and Oliver outside putting twigs on the snow baseball to look like stitches. Ava and Ollie had brought as much light to his grandpa as they had to him. If only he could find a way to convince her to stay.

She stirred and put her fake smile on her face. "It smells delicious in here." The woman was no stranger to hiding what she was going through. He only wished she knew she didn't have to.

"They're outside finishing the snow baseball. I'm in charge of not letting you look until Oliver is ready."

Her smile transformed to a genuine one at the mention of her son and his project. "He's been looking forward to making that since he saw the first snowflake."

"I took some pictures of them making it earlier. I'll text them to you."

"Thank you. I'll treasure them." Sadness washed over her face, but vanished when Oliver opened the front door and said he was ready. She led Max and Zeus out the door.

"Wow, this is amazing!" She pulled out her phone and took pictures from different angles. "It's the best snow baseball I've ever seen."

Max reached out for her phone. "How about a mother-son photo?"

"Sure!" She ran over and posed proudly with Oliver, then gestured to Vernon to trade places with her. "I need some with the two artists."

Oliver soon waved Max and Ava back over. "Now we need one with all of us. Come on, Zeus!"

They all followed the boy's instruction, then Max clapped his bare hands together, as much to warm them as to get everyone's attention. "Who's hungry?"

Ava raised her hand. "I am, and I can't wait to taste those Sloppy Joes!"

Gramps puffed up his shoulders. "Our snow baseball maker is also becoming quite a chef. Oliver, lead the way and let's eat."

Ava once again encouraged the stories Gramps told over dinner, and Max prompted as many as he could think of involving Colette, her late husband, and Jack. He didn't know if he could stop her from leaving, but he would make sure her note cards were as full as they could be.

She insisted on helping with the cleanup from dinner, so Max and Oliver took Zeus outside for some quick drills. When they brought the dog back inside, the last dishes were being placed into the cupboard.

Gramps pulled Ava into a firm hug. "I hope to see you again, dear Ava. It's been a pleasure to have you two here this week."

She squeezed him tightly. "The pleasure has been all ours, Vernon. Thank you for being so welcoming to us and for all you've done with Oliver." Her eyes were full of longing when she watched him hug Oliver goodbye and go upstairs to bed.

Max put his arms around Ava and Oliver. "Let's go sit by the fire."

She let him lead them into the living room, then sat on the chair next to the couch. Oliver sat on the floor next to Zeus. "Sweetie, maybe you could read a book to Zeus. I'll bet he's a great listener."

The boy grinned and pulled a book out of his bag. When Max tossed a pillow to him, he curled up next to Zeus and started reading.

Max walked over to the desk and pulled out a notepad and pen, then handed them to her. "In case you learned anything new at dinner."

She smiled broadly at him. "Thank you."

He tried to ignore the shivers she sent down his spine when she looked at him that way. He tended to the fire, taking his time arranging the fresh logs so she could write, and wishing the family scene that was playing out could last.

She continued writing after he sat down on the couch. While Oliver's voice got quieter and he fell asleep, Max watched her, enjoying the glow the light from the fire cast on her delicate features and thinking how natural it was to have her there. She wrote quickly, as if she had to write things down before the memories disappeared.

He wondered if he should be taking his own set of notes. Strong, beautiful, vulnerable, determined . . . he didn't need notes to remember everything about her. Unforgettable women had an effect on a man that didn't fade with time.

He gestured toward Oliver. "How about if I take him someplace more comfortable?"

"Sure, thanks."

Max carried Oliver up to the guest room. After covering him with the comforter, he prayed over him. His eyes stung when he looked at the sleeping child one last time and left the room.

When Max sat back down, she set the paper aside and smiled at him.

"Did you get everything?"

"I think so."

He gestured to the open space on the couch next to him. "Why don't you come over here and make some new memories with me?"

She looked at him like he had just suggested they rob a bank together. What had suddenly changed between them? Had she forgotten the kiss they had shared at Colette's? His pulse still hadn't returned to normal from it. "What am I missing?"

She tilted her head, sending her silky hair over her cheek and making him want to bury his hands in it and kiss her senseless. "Max . . . you know there can't be anything between us." The sadness in her eyes only served to add to his confusion and frustration.

"There's already something between us."

"But it can't be."

"You're not leaving yet. Give me tonight to convince you to stay."

"You know it's not just because I'm leaving." She stood and walked to the fireplace, wrapping her sweater close. When he met her there, she tried to step away.

He caught her in his arms and pulled her against him. "You know there's something here. Something real."

She pushed against his chest. "Max, what are you doing?"

His voice was raw with emotion. "I'm trying to show you how I feel."

"But we're cousins!" She released herself from his grasp and stepped back.

He dropped his arms as a laugh burst out of him. "We're what?"

She turned, but not before he saw the pink rise in her cheeks.

He reached out and circled her waist before she could get away. "Where did you get that crazy idea?"

"Isn't Colette your aunt?"

"Would I be doing this if she was?"

She relaxed against him and searched his eyes. "We're not related?"

"Not in the least. Our families are close, but we're not related in any way."

She laughed with him and covered her red face. "Thank God. I was feeling like a horrible person for having the best kiss of my life with my cousin."

"Best kiss of your life, huh?" His heart raced as he pulled her closer. "Let's top it."

She grinned in answer and tilted her mouth toward his. When their lips met in a very non-cousinly way, he knew he couldn't let her leave—not without a fight.

Chapter 31

AVA HAD NEVER FELT so alive. Being in Max's arms and holding no secrets from him was pure heaven.

Without taking his arms or his lips from her, he walked backward to the couch and pulled her onto his lap. It was the closest thing to perfection she had ever experienced with a man. She wanted to stay there with him forever.

He was everything she had ever wanted in a man—tender, strong, sweet. It was no wonder she was losing her heart to him.

Who was she kidding? It was already lost. She broke the kiss and rested her head in the hollow of his neck as she caught her breath.

His voice was rough as he whispered in her ear, "I'm glad we're not related."

Their eyes met as they laughed together. "No more glad than I." She met his lips again with hers, taking everything she could and storing it in her heart. Leaving him was going to be the worst thing she had ever had to do.

Leaving. Her heart ground to a halt. No matter how much she wanted to stay, she couldn't invade Jack's life. She still had to leave his town. Their meeting had proven that much.

What was she doing? She and Max couldn't have a future, and every moment she spent with him made her want that future more. She drew out of the kiss again, her decision made. "We have to stop. I'm leaving tomorrow."

"Tomorrow?" His eyes met hers and gazed straight into her soul. "Stay here tonight."

Warmth flooded her. If there was ever a time she could fall to temptation, this was it. *Lord, please give me strength.* "You know we can't."

His face flushed. "As much as I would love to have you in mine, I meant in the guest room. Oliver is already asleep in there, and I don't want to miss a minute with you."

She nodded. If she was leaving tomorrow, they had precious few minutes left. "I don't want to miss a minute, either."

He broke into a grin. "You'll stay?"

"I'll stay. I can't stay like this, though." If she didn't get off his lap, it was going to be impossible to go to the guest room.

"I can't either." He let her go, and she moved to the spot next to him, nestled under his protective arm. They sat quietly and she savored the feel of him next to her and the crackling of the fire. As Bing Crosby softly crooned *I'll be Home for Christmas* on the radio in the corner, her senses were washed over with peace.

Sitting with his arm around her and watching the fire brought a different temptation, one far stronger than mere physical desire. She wanted to stay there with him forever, to make his home hers. To have a family and build a life together. Now that he knew everything about her, she felt even closer to him.

She realized she still didn't know everything about him. As good as it felt having him know her wounds and secrets, she needed to know his. The memories she was storing up were going to have to last forever, and she didn't want to miss a detail about him. "You owe me a story."

He looked down at her. "I do?"

"You said you would tell me what brought you to Summit County when I told you what brought me."

His body tensed next to her. "You're right. I do." Everything about his expression changed, and she knew she was about to learn his deepest wounds. "You're sure you want to know? It's not pretty."

"I want to know everything about you." She needed to know. Words and memories were all she would have left of him when she returned to her own life in Miami.

She interlaced her fingers with his and waited.

He looked into her eyes for a long moment before beginning. "I told you that I came here five years ago to get a fresh start and to help Gramps after his heart attack." He rubbed his hands on his jeans. "All that is true, but I needed the help more than he did."

He stood and paced the room. It was as if his body was fighting against the revelations that were coming.

When he stopped in front of the fireplace, she joined him there and wrapped her arms around his waist. "There's nothing you can say that will change how I feel about you."

He gripped her so tightly she could barely breathe. After a moment, he released her and stepped back to look into her eyes. "What if I told you that I almost got a bunch of people killed—cops, civilians, Zeus, and myself?"

Chapter 32

MAX WATCHED AVA'S FACE for her reaction. The compassion there made him wish he could take back his promise to tell her everything.

"What happened?"

He led her back to the couch, where she sat facing him. It was always a risk telling the story, which was why the only people he had shared it with were his immediate family, his pastor, and a couple of people at the station. As much as he didn't want to let her see his weakness, he needed her to know all of it.

It never got easier to tell, but he knew how to tell it and how to make it quick. "I was at an all-time low. I hated my job, myself, and my life. My head wasn't in my work." He didn't know at the time that he was about to learn how much lower he could go.

"I was part of a task force that was working on busting a group of drug traffickers in Flint that had ties to a major cartel. They had a plant on our task force who spied on us and kept them one step ahead of us for months." He shook the memory from his mind, reminding himself that he didn't need to return to the scene to describe it.

"We were getting close to making a huge bust that would crush their operation, and they came up with a plot to blow up an entire city block that included the offices that held the task force." It still made him angry—and guilty—to think about how close they had come. "If their plan had succeeded, it would have killed a lot of innocent civilians, including children."

"It sounds like what happened in Oklahoma City all those years ago."

He nodded. "Their plan made Oklahoma City look like a pack of firecrackers. The reason for making it a big explosion was to make it unclear what the target was and point suspicion toward a militia group instead of them."

She shuddered but didn't move from her position. "You obviously stopped it, or I would have heard about this."

"We stopped it. Officially, I stopped it." His gut clenched. He hated this part of the story. "They gave me a challenge coin and called me a hero." The words tasted bitter on his tongue.

"Then why do you look so miserable?"

"Because I know better."

She winced at the hardness in his voice but never dropped his gaze.

"I dropped the ball, and I missed signs that were right in front of my face. By the time I saw clearly, it was almost too late to stop it." Owning up to his own mistakes never got easier. "If I would have had my head in the game—if I wouldn't have been played for a fool—I could have prevented them from getting as close as they did."

"Oh, Max. How could you have prevented it?" She scooted closer and took his hand.

He jerked it away. Her sympathy only made him feel worse. "If I hadn't ignored my gut and the signs that were right in front of me, I would have seen the plant for what she was."

Her eyes widened. "Oh." She seemed to understand what he was telling her without him having to explain it. "You were involved with her?"

Involved. It sounded almost quaint. There was nothing quaint about sleeping with the drug boss's secret mistress and being manipulated by her like a trained dog.

"I wasn't the same man then." He leaned forward and rested his arms on his knees as he stared into the fire. "As a cop on those streets, I had seen so much of the worst in people—child abuse, sexual assault, murder, all of it. I felt stained by it all. Everything I had believed and the way I had lived my life didn't fit with what I saw as reality. I had all but disowned God by then." He couldn't look at her. The man he was back then wasn't worthy to be in the same room with a woman like Ava.

She didn't back down. "And this woman?"

"We were practically living together. She had more access to the task force's information from talking to me at night than from working with us during the day." He turned back to Ava. She was looking at him with the same compassion she had before. This time, instead of spurring his shame, it fueled him. "The day of the planned bombing, she stayed home, claiming she was sick. She said goodbye as if it was any other day when Zeus and I walked out the door. If I hadn't taken cold medicine back to her twenty minutes later, I wouldn't have overheard the phone conversation she was having when I came in. She was too busy gloating to hear me, so I snuck back out the door and called the task force commander. He called for the raid, and we got to their headquarters within minutes of their planned time to leave. It was a miracle that none of our men died in the raid."

"But that's when you and Zeus were hurt?"

He looked over at the dog sleeping peacefully on his cushion. "When Zeus lunged at the guy who had a gun pointed at my chest, he flinched. The bullet grazed Zeus's leg on its way to my side. The next thing I knew, I woke up in a hospital room with my parents and Gramps standing over me, praying together." He finally looked her in the eye. "It took some time to see God's hand in all of it, but He saved me in more than one way that day. A few weeks later, when I was healed enough to get around but hadn't been cleared to return to work, Gramps had a heart attack. I came here to help him and keep him company. We recovered together, and after a long walk in the woods, I decided I never wanted to go back to Flint. I told God then and there that I would never question Him again—and that I would never ignore my gut instinct."

She wrapped her arms around his shoulders. "I'm so glad He protected you that day."

Chapter 33

DESPITE STAYING UP AND talking with Max into the early morning hours, Ava woke feeling more rested than she had since she'd arrived in Michigan. With her eyes still closed, she inhaled deeply, savoring the faint scent of Max's aftershave that lingered on the shirt he had given her to sleep in. It offered as much comfort as the old bed and warm quilt.

Max and Vernon's muffled voices below her brought her fully out of her slumber. Oliver wasn't in the bed, so he must have gone downstairs already. She stretched and pulled the thick comforter around herself. *Just one more minute.* She looked around the room to absorb every detail of it, just like she had everything else since she'd fallen in love with Michigan, Max, and her family.

Her heart dropped when she looked at the clock. There wasn't much time before she and Max had to leave the house in order for him to get to work on time. He was going to take her to her car, which she had left in Colette's parking area in her haste to get away from Jack, the shop, and her own sense of failure.

She quickly changed out of his shirt and into her own clothes, inhaling his scent one more time before neatly folding it and setting it on the bed. She ambled downstairs and found Max and Vernon in the kitchen. Max was tending to sausage patties while Vernon fried eggs next to him.

Max gave her a sleepy smile and heart-stopping wink when he looked up and saw her standing there. "Morning."

"Morning. Good morning, Vernon."

"Good morning, Ava. I was happily surprised to hear that you and Oliver were our guests last night. How do you like your eggs?"

She walked over to peer at the stovetop. "What's your specialty?"

"Over medium."

"Perfect, then that's how I like my eggs. Where is my little man?"

Max gestured toward the living room with his spatula. "He's in with Zeus."

She padded into the living room, where Oliver was trying to get Zeus to roll over. He ran to her, hugged her, then ran back to the dog's side, so she returned to the kitchen. "Can I do anything?"

Just then the toast popped up. Max tilted his head toward the toaster. "Perfect timing. Would you like to butter that?"

It felt good to be part of such a simple activity. Sharing meals and kitchen chores with the two men during the times that she and Oliver had been their guests had filled something deep in her heart. Today she didn't feel like a guest. She felt like family. Like she belonged there.

Why did she have to go? Why would God finally allow her to find love—and two families—in a place she had to leave?

God didn't force her to fall in love with Max—or to make the trip to Michigan. Had she ignored His warning? She didn't think so, but she needed to make sense of it somehow.

She pushed the thought from her mind. There was less than an hour to make memories with Max. She needed to make the most of the time they had before it was too late.

After Oliver washed his hands, he sat at the table. "Do we live here now?"

"No, we still live in Florida." She ruffled his hair, but he kept his head focused on his plate.

With every silent minute that passed during breakfast, she felt the tension rise from Max's side of the table. She had caught him staring at her more than once, the pained look in his eyes echoing the hurt in her heart.

He hadn't even eaten half of his food when he stood and took his dishes to the sink. "I need to leave earlier than I thought."

"Sure, I can be ready as soon as you need." Was he now in a rush to get rid of her? She couldn't blame him if he was. It was excruciating knowing that their goodbye was coming. It would be a relief to have it over with.

She reached for Oliver's empty plate. "You're going to stay here with Mr. Vernon and Zeus while I get my car and our stuff from the hotel room."

Oliver's eyes danced. "Are we going to stay the night here again?"

"No, sweetie." She blinked away the tears that threatened and put on the most convincing upbeat voice she could muster. "We're going to go home. Are you excited to see Auntie Sarita and Uncle Enrique and the kids?"

His eyes filled with tears. "No! I don't wanna leave here!" He ran to Max, who immediately picked him up and held him.

When she started to follow, Vernon stood and put his hand on her arm. "You two go ahead. I'll take care of clean up and Oliver."

"Oh, Vernon, no. I can—"

"Thanks, Gramps." The tension was thick in Max's voice as he set Oliver down and strode quickly toward the coat rack.

Vernon hugged Ava. "I'll take care of him and we'll see you when you get back." He turned quickly, and she wondered if his eyes held the mist hers did.

She almost had to run to catch up with Max when she walked out of the house after reassuring Oliver. Max avoided her gaze when he held the passenger door open for her. Had she made him angry?

The drive through Lakes End was quiet, and she watched solemnly as workers strapped fresh-cut Christmas trees to the light posts in town. Her eyes stung as she saw the evidence of something else she would miss in this place. Spending Christmas here with Max and Colette . . . Vernon . . . Kara . . . It would be a dream.

Her stomach tensed as she felt the unfairness of what was happening. Why did she feel so obligated to stay far away from Jack Sullivan? It wasn't like they had any kind of relationship apart from DNA. Could they actually coexist together and keep their secret?

No.

She couldn't keep lying to Colette. It was time to go, before any more damage could be done.

But what about the sense of family—of belonging—that she felt with Max and Vernon?

Chapter 34

MAX PULLED INTO THE parking spot next to Ava's car. Neither had spoken on the ride, and he wondered if she was as torn up as he was. Saying goodbye to Oliver had been sheer torture, and he wondered if he would ever see the boy again. Judging by the occasional sniffle from her side of the car during the ride, he wasn't alone in his misery.

His agony had been growing since they sat down to breakfast and she made it clear that nothing he'd said last night had changed her mind. The house had felt complete with her and Oliver there, and the knowledge of them leaving was tightening a vice around his chest.

So was anger. All it would take was a word and she could put a stop to both of their suffering. She was a grown woman, and she didn't have to hide from Jack. He parked the car and looked at her. "You're really going to leave?"

"You know I don't have a choice."

He gave her a hard look. "No, I don't know that."

"For what it's worth, I hate leaving you."

The redness around her eyes only made him want to fight harder to keep her there. "Ava, I'm falling in—"

She silenced him with her finger. "Please don't say it. It will only make this worse."

He gripped her hand in his. "Whether or not I say the words, you know it's true. And you feel the same."

Tears spilled over her eyes when she nodded.

His voice was hoarse as he pleaded, "What can I do to make you stay?"

"You know I can't stay. I want to, but—"

He silenced her with his kiss. Just as she wouldn't let him tell her he loved her, he wouldn't let her tell him goodbye.

The kiss said both, and he took his time to get his message across. This might be their last moment together, and he wasn't going to let her go without showing her how he felt—or reminding her that he wasn't alone in it. She clung to him fiercely, responding to his every move with one of her own.

They both gasped for breath at the same time. He couldn't come up with a single word to say as they held each other.

It was up to her now. He wasn't too proud to beg, but he knew a losing battle when he was in one.

She kissed his cheek as she pulled away from him. When he opened his mouth to speak, she shook her head and scrambled out of the car.

He buried his face in his hands. How had this happened so fast? He had sworn off women after the debacle with Cecilia. How could Ava go from a stranger to the woman he couldn't imagine spending the rest of his life without in such a short time?

He wasn't going to let her stop him from telling her, from saying something. He needed to look into her eyes and hold her one more time.

When he opened his eyes, determined to make a last-ditch attempt, she was gone. The parking lot was as empty as his chest.

~eee~

Max's finger hovered over his phone. Conversations with Ava over the week and a half since she'd been gone left him frustrated and exhausted. Part of him didn't want to call, didn't want to push through another night of small talk in an effort to stay connected when she was determined to stay in Florida.

One of these nights he would force himself to stop calling, but not tonight. Not on her birthday. He hit Send.

"Hey."

His heart calmed at the sound of her voice. This was why he called. That voice reached into the inner recesses of his being. "Happy birthday. Did you get the gift I sent?"

He heard the catch in her voice. "I'm looking at it right now. Thank you."

"I framed one for myself too." He looked over at the photo on the mantel, the smiling faces surrounding the snow baseball hitching his gut. "Oliver looked so proud."

"He insisted on putting it up in the hotel room under the puny plastic tree."

Looking over at his own tree, cut from the back end of the property, did nothing to fill him with Christmas spirit. "There's plenty more snow here. Anytime he wants to come make another one . . ."

Ava cleared her throat. "We celebrated my birthday tonight at Sarita's. Oliver's gift for me was a piñata."

He wasn't surprised that she had changed the subject. Every conversation seemed to go this way lately. "Did he let you use his baseball bat to hit it?"

"Of course." Her voice sounded relieved. "I think that was just his excuse to take it to the dinner."

So we're not going to talk about anything real tonight. Again.

He played along. "He's a smart kid." It was her birthday. No need to make this yet another painful phone call.

"Tomorrow we're going to the beach with Sarita and the kids."

"Is it warm enough for the beach?"

She finally laughed. "The kids all have sweatshirts. There's no snow on our beaches."

"I saw Colette today. She's glad that we're talking."

Silence. Then sniffles. "She left a voicemail to wish me a happy birthday when I was in the shower. It's the first birthday wish I've ever gotten from a grandparent."

He wished he could be there to put his arms around her and make everything okay. "I miss you."

Silence screamed through the phone. He needed to dial it back. "I'm sorry. I told myself I wouldn't make you feel bad on your birthday."

"Is she doing okay?"

"She's fine. She's keeping the store open until New Year's Eve, then going to Arizona." Should he ask about Jack? No, not on her birthday. He hadn't seen the man since the day Ava's secret came out, and he was certain that Jack hadn't told his family about her. "How did your meeting with the landlord and insurance company go?"

"About as expected." The way her voice shook, he could almost hear her tears forming. "They've declared the building unsalvageable, and they're sending me a check to cover the loss of my business."

"I'm sorry I couldn't be there for moral support."

"Me too."

If the building was unsalvageable, she would be getting a fat check to cover the loss of her business. She could start a new one anywhere. "Have you thought about—"

"I'm sorry. I need to go, Max." The line went dead.

Had he pushed her too hard? His frustration had gotten the better of him, but why did she not see the freedom that was right in front of her?

She could open her store anywhere now, but because of her misguided commitment to stay out of Jack's way, she wouldn't consider opening it in Michigan. What was her commitment to Max or the future they both wanted?

He scrubbed his face with his hands. Sensing Max's tension, Zeus was on alert from across the room. "C'mon, deputy. Let's go for a run."

Chapter 35

AVA WATCHED SARITA'S KIDS and Oliver play a game they made up on the beach. It almost looked like a variation of volleyball, but with the rules they made up, it was impossible to follow.

Sarita leaned over and gently bumped her shoulder. "I'm only going to stay quiet for so long, you know."

"I know." She looked at her friend. "I appreciate you giving me some time before you tell me what a fool I'm being."

"You're no fool, Ava." Sarita kept her eyes on the game. "You're making a mistake, though."

"My mistake was going to Michigan in the first place."

"Nope."

Sarita had never held back when she had something on her mind. Her lack of words was as unusual as it was unnerving.

"Go ahead. Say what you're not saying."

Sarita finally turned to look at her. "I'll talk when you're ready to listen."

"Is this some new tactic you're trying with the kids? Because it's sort of terrifying."

"I don't want to waste my words. This is too important."

She was serious. Ava shifted her gaze from the game and faced her. "Okay, you have my full attention. Let me have it."

"Your mistake is bigger than any past or future trip to Michigan. Your mistake is sacrificing your own happiness for something that others have never asked of you." She stared at Ava as if letting the words sink in.

Ava took a deep breath, preparing. "Explain."

"Let's start with your mom. She never asked you to be perfect. I didn't realize that until I became a mother myself. She wanted the normal things parents want for their children, the things we want for those kids playing that ridiculous game, but I don't think she ever demanded what you gave her."

Ava looked at the kids laughing and getting more covered in sand every time they dove for the ball. "No, she wasn't demanding. I wanted to be a good daughter."

"It was more than that." Sarita's tone was kind, but her eyes blazed with passion. "You wanted to be a perfect daughter to make up for the fact that your supposed father was dead. When you found out the truth about your father, instead of being free from making up for a dead man, your chains got heavier. It was as if you completely set your own life on a shelf."

She wasn't wrong. "Maybe a little. I just wanted it to be worth it for her. She gave up her home, her friends, her very identity because of me."

"Wrong."

"How do you figure?"

"She gave up all those things because of her choice. She wanted to be a mother, and she turned her life upside down in order to do so."

"I suppose so. She showed so much love to me that I wanted to return the favor."

Emanuel, Sarita's 3-year-old, ran over to where they were sitting on the blanket and plopped himself on Sarita's lap, covering her with sand. "They're not letting me play."

Sarita gestured to twelve-year-old Carmen and gave her a stern look. "Everyone is playing."

Carmen nodded and walked over to the blanket to retrieve Emanuel, clearly not thrilled with the directive. "Come on, Manny. You're on my team this time."

"Thank you." Sarita wiped the sand off her jeans and looked into Ava's eyes intently. "They owe us nothing."

Ava watched Oliver dive for the ball and get a mouthful of sand. She would never want him to sacrifice his life to make her happy. "You're right."

Sarita raised two fingers. "Which brings me to exhibit number two. Elliott."

Ava's head snapped back at her friend. "What about Elliott?"

"Remember your wedding day?"

Did she ever. "Everyone gets cold feet."

"Everyone doesn't go through with a wedding just because it's been paid for and the guests are already there."

"He was a good man."

"You're doing it again."

"Doing what?"

She let out a sigh and started waving her hands around. "Focusing on everyone else. You married him because he asked you to and your mom loved him, not because you couldn't live without him."

"I did love him. He'd been a good friend to me."

"Don't you want more out of a marriage than a good friend? When he died, you grieved as a friend does, not a wife."

Tears stung Ava's eyes. Tears of guilt. She had tried to love him as a wife, but had failed.

Sarita shuddered next to her. "Do you remember what a basket case I turned into during the hurricane?" When Yolanda hit, Ava and Oliver sheltered in Sarita and Enrique's home because it was farther inland and out of the eye's path. When Enrique left to check on his mother and Sarita couldn't reach him all night, she had paced and cried for hours. She acted like a woman who had lost a part of herself.

At the time, Ava had told herself that the difference between herself and Sarita was that she wasn't an emotional person, that she wasn't a crier. The day she left Max in Colette's parking lot, she found out that wasn't true.

"Let's talk about Jack now. You owe him less than nothing." Sarita's intensity startled Ava. "You don't even know him, and you're ready to give away your future with your dream man because of him. That's just wrong."

"It's not just Jack, though. I can't avoid Colette, and I can't lie to her."

Sarita shrugged. "The way I see it, that's Jack's secret to tell her, not yours. If he doesn't want to know you, let him live his life. But you live yours."

Ava's eyes stung. "I promised from the beginning that I wouldn't blow up his life."

"So instead you're blowing up yours. And Oliver's. And Max's. He calls and texts you every day. Do you really not understand that the guy loves you?" Sarita stood, brushed the rest of the sand from herself, and walked over to her older children to give them a reminder about what it meant to play a game together.

The woman knew how to speak truth.

Another truth hit Ava. She hadn't prayed about it once since she had returned to Miami. She had been so afraid of what God would say that she hadn't let herself listen to Him.

It was time for that to change. *Lord, I'm listening now. Show me who I owe what to.*

Chapter 36

THE COLD AIR BURNED Max's lungs. He had taken Zeus for a longer run than usual, going deep into the woods behind the house in an effort to clear his mind.

They were less than a quarter of a mile from the house when his phone rang. He didn't normally answer his phone on runs, but then he didn't normally get calls from Ava. They hadn't spoken, communicating only through texts, for three days. He slowed to a walk and answered. "Hey."

"Officer Brody."

His body filled with warmth at the playful sound in her voice. She sounded different, lighter.

He could be playful too. "Miss Barton."

The line was quiet. He looked to see if the call had dropped, but the phone showed the connection as active. He walked faster, hoping to get closer to a stronger signal. "Did I lose you?"

"I hope not." Something in her voice gave him hope for the first time since she had left town. "Max . . . do you really think we can make this work?"

His pulse raced. He would do anything in his power to make it work. If it was uncomfortable around Jack, they could move. He didn't care where he lived, as long as he had Ava and Oliver by his side.

He stopped walking and closed his eyes. *Lord, let me get through to her. Bring her back to me.* The words barely made it out of his mouth. "Come home, Ava."

When he heard the snow crunching on the trail ahead, he opened his eyes. There she was, walking toward him with her phone still to her ear and a grin on her face. "I'm home."

He broke into a run, reaching her in seconds. Their bodies met with such force that they fell to the ground together. In spite of their laughter, his lips found hers and let her know just how much he had missed her. When Zeus started barking and pawing at them, their laughter broke the kiss.

"Zeus, sit." He kissed her again to make sure he wasn't dreaming. "I can't believe you're here."

"Sarita and God both gave me a talking to, and I'm here."

"I'll be sure to thank them both." He looked around. "Where's Oliver?"

"In the house. Your grandpa was kind enough to ask him to help get dinner started so that I could come out alone."

"I'll be sure to thank him too."

Her expression grew serious and she cupped his face. "I love you."

"I love you too. More than I ever thought I could."

She kissed him again. It was real. She had come back to him. For the first time in two weeks, he felt happy.

The snow started seeping through his pants. She was probably freezing. He stood, bringing her with him, and kissed her again for good measure.

She shivered as she wrapped her arms around his waist. "You'd better take me inside or you're going to have a frozen Floridian on your property."

"I'll take you anywhere you want to go."

Chapter 37

AVA CLUTCHED THE WARM mug in her hand as she watched Max add wood to the fire. She still hadn't warmed up after changing out of her wet clothes and into dry ones, but the Christmas tree, fire, blanket, and tea were helping.

So was being with Max. Everything about being back in his home made her feel that all was right in the world. Oliver's squeals and Zeus's happy barks in the back yard added to the perfection of the moment. She let thoughts of her business and the Sullivan family retreat to the back of her mind as she basked in the glow of her surroundings.

When he returned to sit next to her on the couch, she held the blanket up for him to join her under it. She shivered as he put his arm around her.

"We need to get you some warmer clothes."

"We do." Despite putting her jeans over her yoga pants and layering a t-shirt under her sweater, she was still cold. "In the meantime, you're going to have to keep me warm."

He grinned at her. "Your wish is my command."

"I like the sound of that. I wish for a kiss."

He obliged, making her wish they could stay just as they were forever.

She was reminded that they weren't going to be alone for long. "We probably shouldn't be making out here when your grandpa and my son come back inside."

"Probably not. I don't think they're coming back in anytime soon though. I think Gramps is giving us some alone time. Plus, he missed Oliver."

"He's such a sweet man." She rested her head on Max's chest and breathed in his scent that she had missed so much. "I'm so happy to be back here with you."

"Me too. I hated being here without you." He kissed the top of her head. "Speaking of that, I'm afraid to ask if you're here for a short visit or for good."

"That depends largely on you." She couldn't make any assumptions, especially after she left him for two weeks.

"I'll do as much begging as it takes to keep you and Oliver here forever."

She released a breath in relief. "I like the sound of that."

He laughed. "Of me begging?"

"No. Staying here forever."

"Me too." He tightened his hold on her. "There's a ring around here somewhere that would look lovely on your finger, but we'll talk about that when you're ready."

If she could, she would accept the ring right then and there. There was too much to figure out first.

Max's breath was warm on her neck. "What about Jack?"

"I really don't know." She set her tea cup down so she could snuggle closer to him. "All I knew when I packed my car and started driving north was that I needed to be with you and give being happy a try."

"I like that. Did you tell Colette you were coming back?"

She shook her head. "I didn't tell anyone anything. I was afraid that if I thought too long about it, I would get overwhelmed and change my mind. I just threw everything in the car and drove here."

"And now that you're here?"

"I don't think I'm ready to see anyone just yet. It's going to be hard to see her and continue to keep this secret from her, but it needs to be up to Jack whether he shares it with his family." She had been reminding herself for days that the Sullivans, including Colette, were Jack's family, not hers.

"It will be easier to stay under the radar if you two stay here." His lips twitched into a grin. "Small town and all."

She laughed at his failed attempt to keep a straight face. "Did you just take advantage of my awkward and painful family situation to get me to stay here with you?"

"Absolutely. Did it work?"

"We'll stay tonight and I'll figure out what I'm going to do tomorrow." There was too much to think about tonight. She just wanted to enjoy being with Max in his home.

He tipped her chin to look into her eyes. "You don't have to make those decisions alone anymore. We'll figure things out together and do whatever is best for you and Oliver. If you don't want to stay in Summit County, we can go somewhere else."

Sarita was right. He was her dream man. "That would uncomplicate the Jack situation, but this place feels like home. It did before I ever realized who Colette was. Oliver and I both want to be here. With you."

"What about work? Is everything settled with the store?"

"Yes. I have a full bank account that will allow me to open another one wherever I want." Thinking about all the details involved in starting a shop made her tired. "It's a lot of work to start something new, so I may just live off the settlement until Oliver starts school and get a job with someone else. It's on the list of things to figure out."

He squeezed her closer. "Together."

"Together." When she looked into his eyes, thoughts of work and Jack and what the future held disappeared. Only Max and the life they could create remained.

The back door banged open and they separated. "Mommy, Officer Max! Zeus rolled over for me!"

She rose from her seat to help Oliver out of his winter gear. "What do you think about staying here with Officer Max and Mr. Vernon for a couple of days before we go back to the hotel?"

"Cool!" Once free of his boots, he scrambled over to throw his arms around Max's legs.

Vernon kissed Ava on the cheek. "You can stay as long as you like, honey. Oliver, would you like to help me get dinner for Zeus before we eat?"

Oliver ran to his side, ready to help. He was as happy in this home as Ava was.

Max put his hands on her shoulders, sending warmth through her whole being. "I'll have the concierge deliver your bags to the guest room."

"Can he deliver a shirt that smells like you for me to sleep in?"

"I think that can be arranged."

Chapter 38

MAX PRACTICALLY SKIPPED THROUGH the back door when he got home from work two days later. "Honey, I'm home."

Gramps rolled his eyes, but Ava smiled and offered her cheek for a kiss while she stirred the red sauce in his grandma's favorite roaster. Oliver ran in from the living room and hugged him. He had only been greeted this way twice, but he was sure he could handle it becoming an everyday event.

"I'm sure you won't mind if Oliver and I take Zeus out before dinner, Maxwell." Oliver ran to put his boots on, and the gleam in Gramps' eyes let Max know that he was enjoying having houseguests too.

"Thanks, Gramps."

"Treat her like a lady while we're gone."

Max held up three fingers. "Scout's honor."

Ava turned down the stove and set the wooden spoon aside. By the time she turned, he was there to capture her into his arms and give her a proper kiss. He let his lips do his communicating, but kept it brief so that he could follow through on his promise to Gramps. "This kitchen is better with you in it."

She reached back and picked up the spoon, dipping it into the sauce before holding it in front of him. "Vernon showed me how to make your grandma's red sauce. Taste."

It was perfect, as was the Cuban meal she'd made last night. "Delicious. You're going to spoil me."

"I'm going to try."

"What did you do today while I was at work missing you?"

"We put up the rest of the Christmas decorations, and I helped your grandpa sort through some things of your grandma's. He said he needed a woman's perspective to help him decide what to keep and what to donate."

Max had wondered what would happen if he got serious about a woman while he was living with Gramps. It hadn't occurred to him that he could find someone who would treat him as if he were her own grandfather. "Thank you. You're wonderful."

She winked before turning back to the stove. "That's what he said, too."

He fought the temptation to kiss her until the smoke alarm went off. Instead of burning the house down, he reached into the drawer for silverware and started setting the table.

She turned and leaned against the counter. "I called Colette today."

"Did you tell her you're here?"

"No. I decided to surprise her at the store tomorrow."

"She'll love that. You're ready for it?"

She nodded. "I'm ready. I miss her."

"What about Jack?"

"Hopefully he won't drop by while I'm there. If he does and I have the chance, I'll assure him of my discretion." She dropped her gaze. "There's nothing else I can do."

He rejoined her and wrapped his arm around her waist. "Is that sadness about Jack or about keeping something from her?" The sound of the back door opening and Zeus's nails on the wood floor ended their conversation, and he wondered about the answer through dinner.

—*ele*—

The next afternoon, Max was paying for his lunch at Anchor's when Jack walked into the restaurant. They hadn't seen each other in over two weeks, since the day Max confronted him in Colette's store, and Max raised his hand in greeting.

Jack eyed him warily, as if wondering if he was going to be accused again, but nodded in his direction. He sat alone in one of the booths that lined the wall, so Max strolled over to it. "May I join you for a minute?"

He gestured to the seat across the booth, but didn't look happy about it. Seeing the shadows under his eyes, Max wondered if he had lost sleep over Ava's revelation.

"Jack, I owe you an apology for the last time we spoke."

He just nodded, but he studied Max's eyes.

Max fidgeted with the gloves in his hand. "I was out of line, and I didn't know what I was talking about."

His eyebrows rose. "And now you do?"

"Now I do. She told me."

Jack's shoulders dropped. The man looked like he was carrying the weight of the world.

"I'm sorry, Jack. Is there anything I can do?"

He cleared his throat and kept his voice low. "Can I count on your silence?"

"Of course. Neither Ava nor I have told anyone."

"I'm still not sure what to do about it. I have a family to consider." He leaned forward, keeping his voice low. "I haven't even been able to tell Amanda yet. She's exhausting herself going back and forth to her parents' house, and I haven't wanted to lay this on her too."

Max was reminded that Jack was the good man he'd always thought him to be. It was clear that he was taking great pains to do right by his family. "You have one of the best families I know. If you decide to tell them, they'll understand. It's not like you did anything immoral."

Jack shook his head. "I didn't think so at the time. Now I wonder."

"Whether or not you tell your family is your call. I'm the only one Ava has told, and she's not going to say anything to anyone."

"You're sure about that?"

Max nodded. "She wasn't planning to tell anyone, even you. The only reason she told you was because she didn't want you to think she was a crazy stalker or that your family was in danger."

Just like Ava did with her ring when she was deep in thought, Jack fingered his wedding band. "I wasn't very gracious when—" His head jerked up and shoulders straightened, and he raised his hand to answer Joe Callahan's wave. "I'm meeting with Joe to talk about some houses he's considering flipping. Can we talk about this later?"

"Of course." As Joe made his way to the booth, Max stood. "We're both praying for you."

Jack reached out his hand to shake Max's. "I appreciate that more than I can say."

Max greeted Joe quickly and headed out the door. The brisk air caught in his lungs as he typed out a text to Ava, letting her know that Jack was just starting a business lunch. He prayed for Ava's time at Colette's store, then for Jack and Ava. "Thy will be done" prayers were always easiest when he had no idea what to ask God to do.

Chapter 39

THE TENSION—some of it, anyway—left Ava's shoulders when she saw Max's text. She still had to keep a secret from someone she loved, which never felt right, but at least she didn't have to worry about running into Jack today.

As they walked down Main Street, Oliver skipped beside her, trying to keep snowflakes from falling into his art bag. "Do you think Santa knows I don't have a backpack anymore?"

Yolanda was certainly thorough in her destruction. For all Ava knew, Oliver's backpack could have landed in Tampa. "Did you add it to your Christmas list?"

"Yeah, but I didn't put it in my letter to Santa. He gave me my gift early, anyway."

"He already gave you your gift?" Ava didn't feed into too much Santa stuff with Oliver, preferring to focus on the real meaning of the season, but she wasn't militant about it. "What was it?"

"Michigan!" He stuck his arms out and twirled around, nearly falling over in the process.

She grabbed the bag before it fell on the snowy sidewalk. "I think God gave us Michigan."

He stopped and took on a serious face. "I know God did, but Santa helps him at Christmas."

She held in a laugh. "I stand corrected."

When they arrived at Up North Clothing and Treasures, Ava held the door so that two women, mother and daughter judging by their almost identical honey-blonde hair, could exit. The store was empty and quiet apart from the soft Christmas music playing. She breathed deeply of the fresh pine branches and winter berries Colette had arranged in the front display. Everything about the place felt festive.

Colette looked up from the sweaters she was folding. "Ava and Oliver!" She crossed the short span between the display and the door. "You came back!"

Ava inhaled the perfume she had missed so much as they hugged. "We're back."

"I knew you wouldn't be able to stay away from Maxwell."

She felt the blood rush to her face as she nodded. "No, I couldn't stay away."

Oliver hugged Colette around her legs. "God and Santa let us come back to Michigan."

She bent over and squeezed him, bringing tears to Ava's eyes. "Your arrival is most certainly an answer to many prayers."

Oliver reached for his bag. "I brought my supplies so I can make pictures for your customers."

Colette beamed at him. "You're hired."

When Oliver let go and skipped toward the sitting area, Colette hugged her again. "I'm so happy you're back. Are you staying at the same hotel?"

"We've been staying with Max and Vernon temporarily, but we'll move to the hotel tomorrow."

Her jaw dropped. "I talked to Vernon this morning, and he didn't say a thing."

"He knew we wanted to surprise you."

"I forgive him then. This is a wonderful surprise." Colette took Ava by the hand and led her toward the chairs at the back of the shop. "If my younger son and his family weren't coming from Arizona for Christmas, I would offer to let you stay with me for as long as you'd like."

"Thank you for thinking of it." Ava tried not to think how wonderful it would be to stay with Colette. "We're used to hotel rooms by now, so it's okay."

"Please sit. I was just about to have some tea, and I even have a juice box for Oliver."

Oliver had set his paper and the new colored pencils Sarita had given him on the table, and he looked like he was ready to get to work. "Miss Colette, where are your customers?"

"Maybe they know I have special visitors right now."

"Oh." He shrugged. "I'll make a picture for you then."

"That would be fabulous!" Colette poured a cup of tea for each of them and sat on the seat closest to Ava. "It's so wonderful to see you. Tell me all about Florida."

"There's not much to tell. I spent most of my time sorting through what little is left of our stuff in the storage."

"Did you get everything settled with your store?"

Ava nodded. "The building was declared unsalvageable. The insurance company counted it as a loss and filled my bank account so I can start over."

"Do you have any idea what you're going to do?"

She forced a smile to her face, pushing aside thoughts about what they had lost to focus on the future ahead. "I'm going to enjoy the holidays and figure it all out in January."

"Are you thinking about staying here after the holidays?"

"That's the plan." Ava sipped her tea. "I need to enroll Oliver in school and find a place to live, but nothing has been decided yet."

The woman leaned closer and lowered her voice. "Might I assume you would only need a place to live for a short time before you and Maxwell come up with more permanent accommodations?"

"You might, yes." Ava couldn't stop her grin. "Neither of us wants to rush things, but since I just turned forty and Max will next year, we don't have much time to add to the family." She couldn't believe she was having this conversation with her grandmother. It felt so . . . normal.

Colette's eyes twinkled as she squeezed her hand. "I don't know why people wait so long these days. Carl and I married two months after we met. Ten months later we had Jack, and a year after that we had Dean." Her voice softened. "I don't regret a moment of it, especially now that Carl is gone."

When Max first told Ava that he had his grandmother's ring but would wait on her timing, Ava had almost proposed to him right then and there. "You're right. Time is precious, and we're old enough to know what we want. That's to be a family."

"I was only seventeen years old, but I knew." Colette shifted in her seat to face Ava. "I hope that whenever you decide to get married, I can be there. Maybe that will take the sting out of not having your mother with you."

Ava's eyes burned when she hugged the woman, though not for the reason Colette thought. "I would like nothing more than to have you at my side when that day comes."

Chapter 40

MAX WAS HIT BY mouth-watering smells when he and Oliver returned from morning drills with Zeus. "What do I smell?"

Ava threw a smile over her shoulder that defrosted him instantly. "Just a little breakfast."

He pulled ice from Zeus's paws while Oliver set the training toys in their bucket by the door and took off his layers of winter gear. "It smells like a feast fit for a king." A savory aroma filled the mud room. Did he also smell pancakes?

"I wanted to do something special as a thank you for letting us camp out here, and since we're moving back to the hotel tonight, consider it our send-off." She tousled Oliver's hair. "Go comb your hair and wash your hands, sweetie."

When he skipped out of the room, Max circled Ava's waist and kissed her cheek. She squealed and wiggled out of his grasp. "Your lips are freezing!"

He grabbed her arm and pulled her back to him. "They need you to warm them up."

She leaned back, just out of kissing distance. "There's a fresh pot of coffee over there. When it warms your lips, you're welcome to try that again."

"Okay, fine." He poured a cup of the hot gold and took a sip. "You know you don't have to go. We have plenty of space here, especially now that you and Gramps cleared out Grandma's old sewing room. Even when my parents get here, we'll have enough rooms for everyone."

"You need time with your family, and we'll be here for some meals. We'll have plenty of time together."

It wasn't the same as having them there early in the morning and late into the evening. He would miss putting Oliver to bed and snuggling in front of the fire with her, talking about their days and dreaming about the future. When he tried another kiss on her exposed neck, she stepped away from him and threatened him with a spatula.

"That's exactly why we're moving out today, mister." The grin on her face belied her words.

He walked over to the fireplace and picked up the ring box he had hidden underneath the garland. Tossing the box into the air when he returned to the kitchen, he grinned at her. "It wouldn't be an issue if you would let me put this on your finger and get Pastor Glenn over here."

When he tossed the box again, her eyes followed it like a cat watching its prey. "Can I see it?" She reached out to catch it, but he grabbed it and hid it behind his back.

"You can see it when you're ready to wear it."

She shrugged and turned back to take whatever smelled so amazing out of the oven. "I saw it when Vernon and I cleared out the rest of your grandma's stuff. I can wait."

If he hadn't seen the sassy grin on her face, he might have taken her seriously. Still, two could play that game. "I guess I could put it in storage somewhere." He turned and took a step toward the stairs.

She grabbed the back of his sweater and pulled him back to her. "Don't take it too far away."

Before he could take advantage of their closeness, Oliver and Gramps walked into the kitchen. Oliver's eyes rounded when he looked at the pan cooling on the stove. "The special egg thingy?"

She grinned at him. "We're having special breakfast today, so I thought we should introduce our hosts to it."

"Cool!" He scrambled over to the table and climbed into his chair.

Ava brought the pancakes while Max carried the egg bake. It smelled amazing, and he could see peppers, bacon, and hash browns peeking out from the cheesy top. "I thought you said you couldn't cook."

"I said I couldn't bake." She winked at him. "I can cook."

Gramps filled everyone's glasses with orange juice. "It seems you can do both now. What are we going to do when you're gone?"

She kissed his cheek before sitting down. "Miss us, I hope."

"No doubt about that. I still expect you to come for dinner every night and stay here Christmas Eve." He sat at the head of the table and nodded toward Max. "Would you like to do the honors this morning, Maxwell?"

"I would." He took Ava's hand in one of his and Oliver's in the other. "Lord, thank you for the people around this table. You have surely blessed this home by bringing Ava and Oliver into it. Please bless this food to our bodies and bless the day ahead." *And please make Ava and Oliver permanent residents of this house soon.*

Ava squeezed his hand before turning her attention to Oliver. "Mr. Vernon has a special surprise for you today."

Oliver looked up at the man who was dishing egg bake onto his plate. "You do?"

"I do. One day a month, some of my friends and I read to young boys and girls at the Senior Center, and today we're having a

Christmas party after the story. Would you like to come with me?"

"Cool!" He almost wiggled out of his seat in his excitement. "Can I, Mom?"

"Yes, you can." She smiled and brushed the hair from his forehead. "Since you're reading, I thought maybe you could count that as school for today."

Oliver threw his fist up into the air. "Awesome!"

Max mouthed to Ava, "New word?"

She grinned and looked to the sky, whispering, "Thank you!"

Max nudged Oliver. "Miss Colette will be there too. She and my grandma started the program when I was your age."

"Really?" The boy started shoveling food in his mouth.

When Max took a bite of the eggs, he wanted to do the same. "This is one of the most delicious things I've ever eaten."

Ava beamed at Oliver. "We've been working on perfecting it for years."

Max tipped his head toward both of them. "I think you've done it."

The rest of the meal passed in quiet, with everyone focused on cleaning every last morsel from their plates. Max looked forward to the time when having meals with Gramps, Ava, and Oliver was an everyday occurrence.

Gramps made quick work of clearing the table and putting away the leftovers while Oliver ran to wash his hands and brush his teeth.

Max turned to Ava. "I guess he likes parties a lot more than school."

"He loved school when it was a building to go to with other kids. It seems that Mom and worksheets are no comparison to a classroom full of children." She handed the bag of candy canes she had hidden in the cupboard to Gramps. "Vernon, thank you for including him today. This will be a real treat for him and will make it easier for me to finish his Christmas shopping."

"The pleasure is all mine, Miss Ava." He looked at his watch. "We'd better go if we're going to be on time."

As soon as Oliver was out the door, Ava turned to the sink and started washing the dishes. Max covered her hands with his. "In this house, the cook doesn't need to worry about cleanup."

She turned that sweet smile on him. "I don't mind."

"Well, I do." He grasped her shoulders and turned her toward the stairs. "Since you've been slaving away in the kitchen all morning and haven't even had time to get dressed, I think it's my turn."

"Okay." She looked down at the sweatshirt she had claimed from his closet that she wore with pajama bottoms. "I don't suppose I should wear this out of the house."

When a knock sounded at the door, Ava sprinted up the stairs. "I'll be down in a few minutes, ready to hit the stores."

"Take your time." Max opened the door and was stunned to find Jack standing on the porch. He glanced into the kitchen to make sure Ava hadn't come back downstairs. "Jack, what brings you here?"

"I wondered if we could pick up our conversation from the other day."

"Come on in." Maybe she would decide to take a very long shower before getting dressed. "Can I offer you a cup of coffee?"

"Sure." Jack stepped through the door, and Max gestured toward the living room.

"Have a seat." When Max went into the kitchen, he typed a quick text, warning Ava that Jack was there. When he brought the steaming cups of coffee into the living room, he handed one to his guest. "You look like you could use this today."

"It was another late night last night." Jack took a long sip of coffee. "I haven't gotten much sleep lately. I thought it might help to talk to you before I talk to Ava."

"I'll help if I can." Max felt compassion for the man. "It's pretty shocking news to get."

"It is." Jack fumbled with his wedding band. "I have questions for Ava, and I'm sure she has questions for me."

Zeus's ears perked up. He looked toward the kitchen, then to Max. Ava must have come back downstairs.

"What's your next step?" Max heard the telltale creak of the floor near the doorway as he waited for Jack's answer.

"I'd like her phone number." His hands seemed to tremble when he took a sip of his coffee. "If you think she wants to talk to me."

Ava offered a slight nod from her spot in the doorway.

Max stood and gestured toward her. "Go right ahead."

Chapter 41

MAX'S QUICK SQUEEZE OF Ava's hand as he passed her in the doorway infused her with the strength she needed to remain standing. Every word she wanted to say drained from her mind as she and Jack stood staring at each other.

Jack cleared his throat. "Can we sit for a moment?"

"Sure. Can I offer you some coffee or tea?" She almost wished Max had stayed to help break the ice.

He lifted his cup. "Got some."

She needed a moment to prepare for this conversation. "Let me just get my tea." After a few deep breaths and a quick prayer, she walked back into the living room and sat on the sofa. Zeus immediately came and stretched out at her feet. "Thank you for coming. I wasn't sure if you would want to talk to me again."

Jack stared into space and twisted his ring. "I don't know quite what to say. I'm at as much of a loss for words today as the last time we talked, but I thought we should try."

She nodded. "I understand. Me too."

"I was just a dumb kid looking for money for Spring Break when I walked into that clinic." He looked at her sheepishly. "It sounded so easy."

She averted her eyes, afraid to see regret in his. "I imagine so."

"I never thought in a million years that anything would come of it. I don't know what I thought."

Catching herself twisting her own ring, she stopped and took a sip of tea. "I didn't come here to ask you for anything, Jack. I don't—" *I don't want anything? That's not really true.* She needed to be honest with him as well as herself. "I came here because I was curious. I wanted to see what you looked like. I wanted to see if I would get any kind of sense about the person you are if I saw you."

"Well," He stood and walked to look out the window. "You probably didn't get a great impression of the kind of person I am when you told me who you were."

"Jack, I've heard enough about you and seen the way you protect your family—"

"That's just the thing." He turned and looked at her intently. "I'm trying to figure out how you fit into my family."

Her nervous laugh turned into a cough. "That's kind of the question of the hour. You don't have—" She cleared her throat. "You don't owe me anything, and you don't have any kind of responsibility—legal, moral, or otherwise."

"That's not completely true." He walked over and picked up Vernon's Bible from the end table. "The Bible says we have responsibilities to others." He turned to face her. "Even if you're not part of the family my wife and I created, at the very least you're one of God's children, and I make an attempt to do right by God's children."

She took a sip of her tea, hoping she would come up with words to say to him. He may be her biological father, but he was a stranger. *Lord, please help us change that.*

He returned to his chair, taking the Bible with him. "Do you believe in the sovereignty of God?"

"I do."

"So do I. He created you using my DNA, and He had a reason for it, just like He had a reason to bring the two of us into each other's lives now." He took a slow sip from his cup. "That means something, even if I don't know what. I know what I want to do, but I haven't even told my wife about it yet."

"Do you plan to—sorry. It's none of my business."

"You're right that I'm protective of my family. I'm treading carefully."

"I'm not a threat to your family, Jack." If she could get one thing across to him today, that was it. "It's your story to tell them if you ever decide to do so, not mine."

He nodded. "I appreciate you understanding that. Can I assume that you haven't said anything to my mother?"

She shook her head. "Of course not. If Colette finds out, it will be because you've chosen to tell her."

"And that's just the thing." He stroked the book on his lap. Maybe he got as much strength and peace from it as she did. "I'm not accustomed to keeping secrets from my family."

Tears stung her eyes. "I'm sorry, Jack. I never should have told you." She never wanted to burden him or his family.

His voice was almost a whisper. "It's a little late for what either of us should have done."

That's an understatement. Please help us, Lord. He's a good man, and I don't want to cause trouble. "I'll respect your wishes, Jack. I didn't come here to blow up your life."

"I appreciate that." He stood and placed Vernon's Bible back on the table. "Can I ask you a favor?"

She stared at his back. He stood just like Oliver. "Yes. Anything."

"It's a lot to ask, but if my mother asks you to come to Christmas dinner with the family . . . would you politely decline?"

A tear escaped her eye, and she wiped it away as quickly as she could. "Yes. Of course."

"I know that you've developed a friendship with her, and I'm not asking you to end that. I would just like to prevent awkwardness or pain at a holiday meal until we get this sorted out." He turned to face her again. "I need some time to figure out how to tell my family."

"Yes. Thank you for not asking me to stop talking to her."

He took a step toward the chair he had been sitting in, but his eye seemed to catch on the mantel. Slowly walking to it and bending toward the framed picture with the snow baseball, his breath caught. "That's your son?"

"Yes." She stepped over to where he studied the boy who had so many of his features and mannerisms. "That's Oliver."

He looked at her, his wet eyes matching hers. "This is a whole lot more complicated than just you and me, isn't it?"

She nodded, unable to speak. What was there to say to make this better?

He took a step and picked up his gloves from the coffee table.

Walking with him to the door, she twisted her ring. When she opened the door, he reached out and laid a hand on her shoulder.

"We'll figure this out, Ava. It will just take some time."

"Goodbye, Jack."

The moment the door clicked shut, she sat back on the couch and buried her head in her hands, finally releasing the sobs that had been building up. Almost instantly she felt the couch move next to her, then felt Max's arm around her shoulders. She turned into his strength. "What have I done?"

* * *

It took hours for Ava to feel like herself again after her awkward visit with Jack, but Christmas shopping was helping. Max turned to her and lifted the overflowing shopping bags in his hands. "We can call it a day if you want. I know your head isn't really in it."

She put on as much of a smile as she could. "No, it's okay. I'd rather be doing this than trying to put on an act for Oliver to convince him that nothing changed today."

"The only thing that changed today is that you finally had the first conversation with Jack."

She looked at him, wanting that to be true. "I want what's best for everyone."

After putting the bags with the others in the back of his car and closing the rear door, Max rubbed her arms. "From what you've told me of the conversation, he wants to do right by everyone as much as you do."

She wound her arms around his waist and laid her head on his chest. "I'm just not sure what that is."

"Forgive me if this sounds selfish, but I think the people you need to take care of first, the only ones you're truly responsible for, are you and Oliver. I want to share in that responsibility, though, Ava."

She looked up into his eyes. "I don't know what I would do without you."

He kissed her temple. "I intend for you to never find out."

Chapter 42

HOLIDAY TRAFFIC WAS PICKING up as Max approached Ava's hotel after work the next day. There had been a smattering of snow overnight, just enough to make everything look fresh and clean but not enough to cause road issues for the people coming into town for the weekend. His parents would be at the house by the time he got there with Ava and Oliver.

When he pulled up to the hotel entrance, they were standing outside waiting for him. *My family.* The thought made his heart skip.

Lord, let us be a family soon. Whatever happens with the Sullivans, don't let that get in the way of what we have.

When Max got out of the car, Oliver yanked on Ava's coat. "Mom, we forgot my seat."

Max opened the back door. "We don't need it anymore, champ."

Oliver looked and saw the new booster seat that Max had picked up when he and Ava were shopping. "Cool!"

Ava rolled her eyes. "So much for him coming up with a different word."

Max chuckled and closed Oliver's door. "We'll work on it."

"If you happen to talk to Santa, please tell him that's on my list."

He opened the passenger door for her and kissed her cheek. "I'll be sure to do that."

The drive was quick, with Oliver telling Max all about their afternoon in the pool. When he pulled into the driveway and saw his parents' car there, his heart jumped up into his throat. Bringing Ava and Oliver to his family felt so right, like all of the pieces of his life were finally in place.

Ava chuckled. "I'm a little nervous."

"Me too. Good nervous." He reached across and took her hand in his. "They're going to love the two of you as much as I do."

"I know I'll love them too." She squeezed his hand. "After all, they raised you."

When they all got out of the car, his mother rushed from the house and threw her arms around him. "Maxwell! You are a sight for sore eyes."

"Hi, Mom." He squeezed her tight, savoring her comforting touch. Letting her go, he gestured toward his guests. "I want you to meet —"

Too late. She was already embracing Ava. "It's so wonderful to meet you. Maxwell and Vernon have told me so much about you." She pulled out of the hug and knelt down to Oliver's eye level. "And you must be Oliver."

He threw his arms around her, obviously seeing that this was how greetings went in this family. "Nice to meet you, ma'am."

"It's wonderful to meet you too." She stood and looped her arm through Ava's. "I hope you're all hungry."

When Max followed them through the door, he was met with a hearty hug from his dad and the unmistakable smell of his mother's chicken and dumplings. He beamed as he watched his parents welcome and accept Ava and Oliver. It didn't just feel like they were welcoming them for dinner. They were welcoming them into the family.

After dinner, Max and his father did the dishes while Gramps and Oliver took Zeus out to run off some steam. The sound of muffled feminine voices in the living room was music to his ears. He'd known the two women would get along famously.

Dad's firm hand gripped his shoulder. "Seems like you've found yourself a keeper there."

He grinned. "I'm sure hoping to."

"You look good, son, like yourself." Emotion clogged the tough man's voice. "It's been a long time."

Max set the cup he was drying in the cupboard. "I feel like myself again. I feel like I've found what I've been looking for."

"Got a ring?"

Max grimaced. "Dad, we just met."

The man arched a brow. "So?"

Max laughed. "Yeah, I've got the ring. It's impatiently waiting on my dresser upstairs, and the second she gives me the go ahead, I'm putting it on her finger."

"That's my boy."

Max felt his mom loop her arm through his, and she rested her head on his shoulder. "She's wonderful, Maxwell. And that little boy thinks you hung the moon and stars."

Max smiled. "The feeling is mutual." Now if he could just get Ava to take her foot off the brake.

Chapter 43

AVA SQUEEZED MAX'S ARM so tightly as they approached Colette's house a few days later that her fingers were losing feeling. The sidewalk seemed a mile long as they made their way to her front door. Thank goodness Oliver was with Vernon and Max's parents for the afternoon.

"It's going to be okay." He stopped beside her, freeing his arm and pulling her to his side. "It's just a little afternoon tea, and they're good people."

"I know." She laid her head on his chest and tried to calm her breathing. "This is just awkward."

"At least Colette will be there." His soothing voice was like salve to her frazzled nerves.

"I know. I think I'm more nervous to see her than I am to see Jack and meet Amanda."

"I'm sure it will be fine. Colette already loves you." Keeping his hand at her back, he nudged her to start walking again. "And when Jack called last night, he said he and Amanda want to get to know you."

Colette's front door opened, and she stood there with a smile on her face and tears in her eyes. Ava finally exhaled. This was Colette, the woman she had developed an instant bond with before she had any idea they were related. She gripped Max's arm as they walked up the steps.

Tears were streaming down Colette's face as she held her arms out to Ava. "My granddaughter."

Ava leaned into her embrace. "I'm so sorry I didn't tell you. I had to let that be Jack's decision."

"I understand. Come in, come out of the cold." She escorted them into the warm home.

Max helped her with her coat then stayed close to her side when they stepped into the living room. With Colette on one side and Max on the other, it felt a little less like the earth was tilting.

Amanda was the first to break the ice, stepping forward and offering a warm handshake to Ava. "It's nice to meet you, Ava."

"It's nice to meet you too." Ava could hear the shaking in her own voice.

Colette poured tea as everyone found seats. Ava was thankful to be able to sit next to Max on the couch. His nearness was keeping her grounded.

Jack cleared his throat. "Thank you for meeting us this afternoon. With my brother and his family meeting with friends, this was the only time we could have privacy."

"Thank you for inviting us." She reached for Max's hand. "It means a lot to me."

Jack and Amanda shared a look before he spoke. "Like I told you on the phone, we would like to get to know you. This is an unusual situation, but you're part of our family now."

Tears sprang to Ava's eyes. When she looked to Amanda for confirmation, the woman nodded.

"Thank you." It didn't seem real, sitting there with her new family. "How are your children taking all of this?"

Amanda spoke for them. "They're all processing it in their own way. We've had a lot of discussions since we told them, and I think it made it less scary that they had all met you and all liked you."

Ava took a slow sip of tea. "I enjoyed getting to know them here on Thanksgiving." She looked at both Jack and Amanda. "You have a lovely family."

"And I hear you have a son." Amanda leaned forward. She seemed as kind and genuine as Ava had heard she was. "Do you have a picture of him?"

While Ava dug out her phone, Colette reached out and touched Amanda's knee. "You're going to love Oliver. He's a treasure."

"Thank you, Colette. He's my everything." When Max nudged her playfully, she smiled at him. "My almost everything."

Jack twisted his wedding band. "Have you explained any of this to him?"

"Not yet." Ava's hands shook as she opened the photo gallery on her phone and handed it to Amanda. "We were talking on the way over here about what to tell him."

Jack chuckled as he looked over Amanda's shoulder at the pictures. "It may be easier than when I explained it to my kids. Less gory details."

Ava winced. "I probably have an easier conversation ahead than you had. He's young enough that I can skip the specifics."

When they laughed together, the tension in the room began to drop. She looked to Max, who smiled and rubbed her back. *Thank You, Lord. This is going to be okay, isn't it?*

By the time Ava had finished her second cup of tea, the awkwardness was gone and she felt for the first time like she hadn't committed some type of crime by coming to Michigan. Even when she noticed Jack, Amanda, and Colette studying her at times, it wasn't uncomfortable. She was studying Jack and Colette too, noting the mannerisms and features that she and Oliver shared with them.

When it was time for everyone to leave, they exchanged hugs instead of handshakes. Ava took extra time hugging Colette. "Thank you for having us, and thank you for not holding it against me that I didn't tell you about all of this."

Colette held her tightly. "I'm glad you let Jack tell me. The Lord worked everything together for good in this." She stepped back and cupped Ava's cheeks. "He knew you needed us and we needed you."

Tears clogged Ava's throat, and she could only nod in answer.

"You'll come for Christmas dinner, right?" The woman looked so hopeful, but Ava had to keep her word.

She swallowed her emotion down. "Thank you, Colette, but I don't think—"

Jack placed a gentle hand on her shoulder and gazed into her eyes. "Christmas dinner is at our house this year, and we would love for you to come."

Amanda smiled at her. "Please come."

"Are you sure?"

"We're sure." He pulled her into an embrace. "You and Oliver are family now."

Chapter 44

MAX DROVE TO THE lake after they left Colette's house, knowing Ava might want a few minutes to gather herself before they headed home. She hadn't said a word since they'd walked out Colette's door.

The wind was whipping, sending snowflakes in every direction around the car. He wondered if that was how her mind felt after the visit. His own thoughts were flying pretty fast too, but he was determined to follow her lead.

He sent his mom a text to see how they were doing with Oliver and find out if he and Ava needed to rush home. Her quick reply, telling him she was helping Oliver finish making some Christmas presents then they were making dinner, filled his heart with warmth. *Please, Lord, if it is Your will, let Ava be my wife and Oliver be my son before next Christmas. Well before next Christmas, if you don't mind.*

Ava reached over and took his hand. "Thank you for going with me today, and for giving me some time to process before we go back to your house."

"Take all the time you need. Was that overwhelming?"

She chuckled. "You could say that. I didn't expect—I guess I didn't know what to expect. I was so afraid that Colette would be hurt that I didn't think about what it would be like to sit with Jack and Amanda."

"I wasn't sure what to expect, either." Jack and Amanda were good people, so he knew they would be kind to Ava, but he had no idea beyond that. "They seem to want to include you and welcome you and Oliver into the family."

"I was hoping they weren't just being polite when they invited us for Christmas dinner." Her voice almost trembled with emotion. "Do you think they meant it?"

He reached across the console to put his arm around her. "I've known Jack my entire life and Amanda since they got married, and I've never known either of them to say something they don't mean. That was genuine."

She leaned into him and took his other hand. "I never thought Oliver and I would be welcomed by two families when we came here." Jack and Ava had both given him permission to tell his parents and Gramps about her parentage, and they had all offered support and prayers.

"I thank God every day that your plan to sneak in and out of town didn't work out."

She laughed. "That plan got derailed at every turn, didn't it?"

He didn't bother hiding his glee from her. "Yes, it did."

"When Jack and I talked at your house, he asked me if I believed in the sovereignty of God." When she turned her head to look into his eyes, hers were shimmering. "Of course I did, but seeing the way He's put all the pieces together to bring Oliver and me here takes it to a whole new level."

"He does know what He's doing. I didn't see it when I woke up in that hospital room all those years ago, but I see it now." *Thank You, Lord. It was all worth it to get here.*

Ava seemed to study him for a moment. Suddenly she straightened in her seat and smiled. "Let's go home."

—ele—

Max watched Oliver through the back window. The boy was becoming a pro at hiding so Zeus could practice recovery in the woods behind the house. He turned and waved to Max, then ran between the trees.

Max whistled to Zeus, who left his spot by the fireplace and trotted to his side. "Let's go find a hiker."

When they walked outside, darkness was starting to settle in. Max led Zeus in random directions for a few minutes to throw him off, but he locked onto Oliver's scent quickly and pulled toward his hiding place.

Oliver giggled and cheered when Zeus found him. "Good job, deputy!"

Max chuckled at Oliver's use of his usual line and gave Zeus his treat. "You both did good." He patted Oliver on his head. "You're a great training partner."

Oliver grinned up at him. "Does that mean I get a treat too? Not a dog treat though. A people treat."

"Your mom is heating up hot chocolate right now. Does that count?"

"Yeah!"

Walking back toward the house, Max threw the ball for Zeus. Each time, the dog took off with Oliver in pursuit.

When they reached the edge of the woods, Ava was walking toward them. "Hot chocolate is ready!"

"You didn't have to come out in the cold to tell us." Not that he stayed cold when she was near.

She shrugged and continued walking. When she got close, Zeus alerted.

Max laughed. "You wanted to be a part of the drills, huh? Show me, Zeus."

Ava stood still with a mischievous smile on her face while Zeus stared at her hip.

Max rubbed his face. "You've got to be kidding me." He would have to talk with her later about putting training items in places that might lead to temptation-inducing contact. A man could only take so much and stay on his best behavior.

Oliver giggled from the sidelines. "Find it, Zeus!"

Max stepped forward and whispered into her ear. "You really shouldn't do this to me."

"We've got chaperones. You'll be fine." Her grin held more than just heat or teasing, something he couldn't identify.

He held his breath as he frisked her, focusing on finding what she had while keeping his hands in respectable places. There must be a bullet, because there was no place to hide anything bigger. "You owe me for this."

She giggled but stood still when he reached into the pocket of her jeans. A bullet was there, as expected, but it felt like there was a string attached to it.

When he pulled it out, something came with it. Something circular. With a stone on it.

It was too dark to see, but he didn't need light to know he was holding his grandmother's engagement ring in his hand. His gaze flew to Ava's. "You know the rule about this, right?"

She closed his hand around it and nodded. "That I can see it when I'm ready to wear it." With a cheeky grin, she stepped back and took Oliver's hand. "Let's go get some hot chocolate before we go back to the hotel."

Chapter 45

THE NEXT DAY, AVA and Oliver packed a bag and moved over to Max and Vernon's for their Christmas Eve sleepover. Ava and Max tucked Oliver into bed in the guest room, reminding him that the sooner he went to sleep, the sooner Christmas day would come. When they got back downstairs, all was quiet except for the crackling of the fire and the soft Christmas music playing.

"Alone at last." Max pulled her close and nuzzled her ear. "Ready to play Santa?"

Leaning into him, she pointed at the tree. "It looks like someone already did. They must have gotten most of the presents out of hiding while we were upstairs." She took a quick inventory and saw that all of the gifts she'd hidden in Vernon's room were artfully arranged around the tree, along with several packages she hadn't seen before.

Max looked at her sheepishly. "In case you hadn't noticed, my family goes a little bit overboard for Christmas."

"I did notice." From the Christmas cookies they had decorated together last night to the feast they had enjoyed at dinner and the extra decorations Max's mother had brought, everything was wonderfully over-the-top. It was so different from the simple way she, Oliver, and her mom celebrated. "Your family is amazing. They make it feel like Oliver and I have been a part of things forever."

"Speaking of that, my mom asked me to give these to you." He handed Ava an unwrapped box. "She didn't want you to feel pressured to keep or use them if you already have some."

Ava opened the lid and saw two stockings, one for her and one for Oliver. "Oh, Max!" Her hand flew to her face. "They're beautiful! Did she make them?"

"Yes. You didn't mention anything about stockings, so I wasn't sure if—"

Ava threw her arms around him. "They're perfect. Ours fell victim to Yolanda, and I forgot to get new ones." She looked up at the fireplace, where two spots waited. She was overcome by the family's thoughtfulness. "This is the best Christmas Eve I could have imagined."

Everything about the day had been perfect. Ava and Oliver helped Colette at her shop, then they enjoyed a traditional Brody Christmas Eve tenderloin dinner once Max's brother arrived. He was as welcoming as the rest of the family, and Ava felt like she and Oliver were truly part of things when they all sat together at the Christmas Eve service. Sitting around the fire together while Vernon read The Night Before Christmas and the nativity story from his Bible was the best ending to the day she could have hoped for. She wasn't even nervous about tomorrow night's Christmas dinner at Jack and Amanda's with the Sullivan and Brody families gathering as one.

Max took the stockings from her and hung them on the mantel. "Is it really the best Christmas Eve you could imagine?" His lips twitched, the way they did when he was fighting a smile. "There's nothing that would make it better?"

"Nothing. It's been perfect."

He shook his head. "Nope. Something's missing."

"What are you talking about?" She looked around the room. Stockings, tree, gifts, even the desk and chair that Vernon had made for Oliver were all present and accounted for.

Max took her hand and drew her near again. "Something's missing for me."

"Ahh, I see." She tilted her head and gave him her best flirty smile. "I suppose you're looking for a Christmas kiss?"

"Better." His voice was suddenly rough with emotion. "I'm looking for a lifetime of Christmas kisses." Without taking his eyes from hers, he bent down on one knee.

A gasp escaped her lips as her hands flew to her cheeks. She hadn't expected him to wait long before proposing, but didn't think it would happen quite so soon.

"Ava, I didn't know what I was missing before you crashed into my life. I want a lifetime of your smiles and snow baseballs. I want to wake up every morning next to you and hear that little boy upstairs call me Dad." With eyes glistening, he held up his grandmother's ring. "You and Oliver are the pieces that have been missing in my life and in this home. If you'll marry me, my Christmas Eve will be perfect."

Her heart filled her throat. Unable to speak, she held her hand out to receive the ring. "You're right. Now it's perfect." When he stood, she pulled him into her arms. "You know what Oliver is going to say, right?"

"Cool!" they said in unison.

Max chuckled. "We need to teach him a new word."

"That sounds like a good job for a dad."

"I'll take it." He stroked her cheek, sending shivers to her fingers and toes. "How about that Christmas kiss now, future Mrs. Brody?"

~ THE END ~

Dear Reader,

I hope you loved Max and Ava (and Oliver!) as much as I do. I got the idea for this book when I heard about a man who had discovered through DNA registries that he had fathered many, many children through his frequent visits to sperm banks as a younger man. Can you imagine? I was completely fascinated by the idea.

Within thirty minutes of hearing about that story, Ava introduced herself to me. If you've ever written a book, you know exactly what I'm talking about. If you haven't, then yes, I'm aware that sounds completely crazy. Max was mentioned in the Summit County Series and had his own story to tell, so they were a perfect match.

If you're wishing you could have seen more of Jack's family reacting to the news that he had another child and seeing those relationships with Ava develop, some of that will be in the next book in the series. Kara's friendship with Ava didn't stop her from feeling like her world had been rocked when she found out she had a sister, and it set some events in motion that led to her making the most impulsive decision of her life. Just wait till you see what she did! I'm working on her story right now, and it's a fun one!

If you've read the Summit County Series, you saw some familiar faces and places in this book. Seeing familiar characters in other books and series is one of my favorite things as a reader, so there will be lots of overlap between the two series. By the way, the Summit County Series is not over. I'm working on the next one right now too.

My newsletter subscribers are always the first to hear about sales and see sneak peaks of upcoming books as well as get some fun bonus content. I'd love to have you join, and there's even a handy QR code at the end of the book to help you with that. I know newsletters aren't for everyone, so if you would just like to be notified of new releases, you can follow me on Amazon or Bookbub, and they'll let you know.

Thank you for spending your valuable time with my imaginary friends. If you would leave a one or two sentence review on Amazon or Bookbub so that other readers can be introduced to this book, I would be so grateful! Reviews are one of the best ways for readers to find new-to-them authors and books. If leaving a review is just too much (I get it - they take precious time that could be spent reading!), but you'd like to leave a rating instead, you can do that, too!

See you in Summit County,

Katherine

About the Author

Katherine Karrol is both a fan and an author of sweet Christian romance stories. Because she does not possess the ability or desire to put a good book down and generally reads them in one sitting, she writes books that can be read in the same way.

Her books are meant to entertain, encourage, and even possibly inspire the reader to take chances, trust God, and laugh at this thing we call life. The people she interacts with in her professional world have absolutely no idea that she writes these books, so by reading this, you agree to keep her secret.

If you want to keep up with her and be the first to know about new releases and sales, join her mailing list by scanning the QR code at the end of the book or emailing her for the link. Newsletters aren't for everyone, so if you would rather just have release announcements, you can follow her on Amazon, Bookbub, and Goodreads. Anytime you would like to chat about your favorite character, share who you were picturing as you were reading, request a story for a special side character, or just talk about books and pretty places, you can email her at KatherineKarrol@gmail.com or follow her on the usual social media outlets.

Also By Katherine Karrol

Hearts of Summit Series

Stay for Love

Summit County Series

Second Chance in Summit County

Trusting Again in Summit County

New Beginnings in Summit County

Taking Risk in Summit County

Repairing Hearts in Summit County

Returning Home in Summit County

Love Remembered in Summit County

Surprise Love in Summit County

Playing Married in Summit County

Let's Be Email Friends

Open the camera app on your phone and aim it here to get a link to
join my email community!
If the QR code is too confusing, just email me for the link :)

Made in the USA
Columbia, SC
09 October 2021